Berkley titles by Peter Brandvold

ONCE LATE WITH A .38
RIDING WITH THE DEVIL'S MISTRESS
ONCE UPON A DEAD MAN
DEALT THE DEVIL'S HAND
ONCE A RENEGADE
THE DEVIL AND LOU PROPHET
ONCE HELL FREEZES OVER
ONCE A LAWMAN
ONCE MORE WITH A .44
BLOOD MOUNTAIN
ONCE A MARSHAL

Other titles

DAKOTA KILL
THE ROMANTICS

ONCE LATE WITH A .38

PETER BRANDVOLD

BERKLEY BOOKS, NEW YORK

ONCE LATE WITH A .38

A Berkley Book / published by arrangement with
the author

PRINTING HISTORY
Berkley edition / October 2003

Copyright © 2003 by Peter Brandvold.
Cover illustration by Bruce Emmett.
Cover design by Jill Boltin.

For information address: The Berkley Publishing Group,
a division of Penguin Group (USA) Inc.,
375 Hudson Street, New York, New York 10014.

ISBN: 0-425-19288-1

BERKLEY®
Berkley Books are published by The Berkley Publishing Group,
a division of Penguin Group (USA) Inc.,
375 Hudson Street, New York, New York 10014.
BERKLEY and the "B" design
are trademarks belonging to Penguin Group (USA) Inc.

PRINTED IN THE UNITED STATES OF AMERICA

10 9 8 7 6 5 4 3 2 1

For my aunts LaVerne and Yvette,
and in memory of Uncle Paul,
with love.

1

IN THE POSH dining room of the Boston Hotel in Clantick, Montana Territory, Sheriff Ben Stillman decided he'd try to enjoy a few minutes of quiet with a cup of coffee and a newspaper. He sipped the strong, black brew and set the cup in the china saucer before him, on the linen-draped tablecloth.

Withdrawing a cheroot from the breast pocket of his shirt, he picked up the newspaper Doc Evans had left on the table when he'd departed a few minutes ago. The doctor and Stillman had eaten lunch with the mayor. Both men were gone now, and Stillman had decided to finish his coffee and read the paper before heading back to the sheriff's office.

It had been a busy week. But then here in the northernmost reaches of Montana Territory, where the outlaws seemed to outnumber law-abiding folks two to one, every week was busy.

It was nearly one o'clock, but the dining room was still abuzz with diners and waiters scurrying about with silver trays. Ignoring the crowd, Stillman scratched a lucifer to life on his thumbnail and lit the cheroot. Blowing smoke, he tossed the spent match into the ashtray, settled back in his chair, and flipped open the newspaper.

He'd read for about five minutes when a formal-looking gent with curly gray muttonchops approached his table.

"Ben, I hate to disturb you," said Leonard Kyle, the, Boston's owner/manager, "but a man has inquired about you. May I tell him you're here?"

"Who is he?"

"Name's Lyle Pettigrew. He just came in on the train. An Easterner, I believe. A writer. He's taken a room here."

"What's he want to see me about?" Stillman asked, taking a thoughtful puff from the stogie.

"He didn't say. I can tell him you're unavailable if you wish. I—"

"No, that's all right," Stillman said, curious. What would an Eastern writer want with the sheriff in a little town like Clantick, Montana Territory? Unless he'd run into trouble on the train . . . "Send him in."

Kyle returned to the lobby, then reappeared in the arched entrance to the dining room with another man at his side. Kyle pointed to indicate Stillman. The other man glanced shyly around the room, worked his mouth as though clearing his throat, and headed for Stillman's table.

What in the hell do we have here? Stillman wondered as he watched the man approach.

Lyle Pettigrew was a dapper little gent with a paper-pale complexion, delicate chin, and weak blue eyes. He wore a pearl-gray derby, matching vest over a white silk shirt, and black coat and trousers with gray pinstripes. His soft, short-heeled shoes were fawn. He wore a flowing black tie. The most delicate pair of pince-nez glasses Stillman had ever seen were attached to the man's lapel by a black celluloid rosette and a length of black ribbon.

"Sheriff Stillman?" the man said as he approached the table. He switched his brown valise to his left hand and extended his right. "I'm Lyle Pettigrew of Brooklyn, New York."

Stillman stood and shook the man's hand. "Pleased to make your acquaintance, sir. What can I do for you? Mr.

Kyle said you came in on the westbound. I hope you didn't run into any problems."

"Oh, no. It was a very enjoyable trip. I did quite a bit of writing, as a matter of fact."

Stillman nodded. "Mr. Kyle also said you were a writer."

"Yes, that's why I'm here." Pettigrew glanced at the table. "Do you mind if I sit down?"

"Not at all," Stillman said, growing a little wary. He'd met a few writers in his day. They were a likeable lot, as long as they weren't writing about *him*. He'd had quite a few newspaper stories written about him when he was a deputy United States marshal, and not one had ever gotten the facts straight. Most writers seemed more interested in telling a compelling yarn than reporting the truth.

Most of the writers he'd met in person had been fairly heavy drinkers and carousers as well, but this man, Pettigrew, didn't look like he drank anything stronger than sarsaparilla. He looked more like an accountant or a Bible peddler.

"Would you like some coffee, Mr. Pettigrew?" Stillman asked when the man had taken a seat across from him.

"That would be nice. Thank you."

Stillman motioned to the waiter, who nodded and disappeared into the kitchen. When he came back with a cup of hot coffee for Pettigrew, the writer spooned several heaping mounds of sugar into the brew, and added several shots of cream. He tasted it, added another shot of cream, tasted it again, and smacked his lips as though pleased.

"Good?" Stillman asked.

"Very good," Pettigrew said, taking another sip.

"So," Stillman said, puffing his cheroot and blowing smoke at the ceiling, "you said your writing brought you to Clantick. Would you mind telling me what story you'll be reporting? I can't imagine anything so interesting in this neck of the woods to bring a man all the way out from New York."

"Well, actually, Mr. Stillman," Pettigrew said, nervously stirring his coffee with a spoon, "it's you yourself that has brought me here."

"Me?"

"Yes, sir. I've been following your career for quite some time. Or at least I was until you disappeared a few years ago. I heard you were shot in Virginia City, by a . . . was it a charlatan?"

"Drunk whore," Stillman said dryly, swallowing coffee. "Shot me in the back by mistake. She was aiming for the cardsharp I was escorting out of the saloon."

"Yes, that was the story," Pettigrew said.

"No, that was my life," Stillman corrected the reporter. "And it ended right there, for a few years anyway. I had to resign my marshal's badge. Doctor's orders and government regulations. The bullet wasn't removable. It's still in there, as a matter of fact."

"What a way for a man like you to be put out of commission. I mean, what irony."

"Tell me about it."

"What brought you back into the profession?" Pettigrew asked, his eyes dropping to the badge pinned to Stillman's blue-pinstriped shirt, half covered by his corduroy jacket.

"A woman," Stillman said, after thinking about it a bit. He smiled. "Actually, it's a long story. I came up here to investigate the murder of my best friend from our hide-hunting days, and ran into a woman I'd fallen in love with several years earlier. She saved me."

Stillman absently rolled the coal of his cheroot against the ashtray, contemplating the lovely French rancher's daughter with the rich, chocolate hair. He'd had the good fortune of making love to her only a few hours ago, when they'd both awakened at dawn. The feel and delectable aroma of her were still fresh on his mind.

He continued. "I'd taken to the bottle before that, and was feelin' sorry for myself. But after I came up here and found Fay again, well . . . everything changed."

Stillman looked across the table and saw Pettigrew furiously scribbling in a notebook he must have produced from the valise open on his lap.

"Hey, wait a minute," Stillman said. "I'd just as soon

you didn't write that down. That was just between you and me."

"Oh, but Sheriff," Pettigrew said, frowning through the pince-nez glasses he'd mounted on his nose, "readers will be most interested in hearing what happened to the fearless Ben Stillman after that fateful day in Virginia City when, for all intents and purposes, you simply vanished."

"Ho, now!" Stillman said, spreading his hands. "I don't want you or anyone else turning my life into a dime novel."

"This won't be just another dime novel, Mr. Stillman, I assure you. While it is true I've made a living—and a quite handsome one at that—writing romantic novels about the West for Eastern audiences, I'd like this project to be different. The real thing, if you will. Nonfiction as opposed to a made-up story. A true and unvarnished portrayal of the wild and woolly frontier."

It was suddenly obvious to Stillman that this Pettigrew was just another Deadwood Dick, an Eastern scribbler who knew very little about the West but who churned out mawkish, sentimental yarns about the region as though he'd been born and raised here. Such books were bound in flimsy yellow covers and often sold in mercantiles and drugstores for ten cents apiece. Stillman doubted that, when it came to life west of the Mississippi, this man knew or appreciated the difference between fiction and nonfiction. That had been made even clearer by the new angle he was already trying to add to Stillman's backshooting debacle.

"If you don't mind me asking, Mr. Pettigrew," Stillman said, suspiciously squinting his blue eyes under a wavy lock of salt-and-pepper hair, "what name do you write under?" He doubted "Lyle Pettigrew" would sell many books.

The writer hesitated. "Why would that make a difference?"

"It might give me a little better indication about what kind of writer you are and what kind of book you would write."

Pettigrew dropped his eyes to study his pencil, and cleared his throat. He mumbled something, but the din in the room was too loud for Stillman to hear.

"Say again?" Stillman urged, leaning forward and cupping his ear.

Again, Pettigrew cleared his throat. More loudly this time, and with an air of self-righteous indignation, he said, "I write under the name Pistol Pete DeFord."

"Uh-huh."

"My stories sell like the proverbial hotcakes, Mr. Stillman. If this one sells even half the copies my last book sold, you could be a moderately wealthy man. Why, you could even give up your job and . . . and, Sheriff, you're not listening."

Stillman's attention had turned to a man walking steadily his way, holding his black bowler awkwardly in his right hand. He was a man of medium height, with dark hair and dark eyes and a neatly-trimmed longhorn mustache. He could have been a drummer of some sort, but for some reason Stillman didn't think so.

As warning bells clanged in the back of his head, Stillman leaned over the table and gave Pettigrew a look of enormous gravity.

"Mr. Pettigrew, I want you to hit the floor when I yell—understand?"

Pettigrew was dumbstruck, thoroughly befuddled. As he bunched his cheeks, his glasses fell off his nose and swung against his coat.

Stillman slid his eyes to the man approaching the table. Suddenly, the man stopped a few feet away and tossed his hat aside to reveal a small, silver-plated pistol. The man extended the gun at Stillman.

"Now! Hit the floor, Pettigrew!" Stillman yelled.

As bewildered as the writer was, he did as he was told. With an indignant grunt, he unseated himself awkwardly, hitting the floor on his side and tipping over his chair in the process.

At the same time, Stillman threw himself to his left. The shooter's gun cracked. Stillman heard the bullet whine past his ear as he hit the carpet. As the gunman swung his weapon to shoot Stillman on the floor, the sheriff clawed his own Colt from his holster and aimed.

The two guns fired simultaneously, making a sound like a thunderclap. Stillman heard the gunman's slug thunk into the carpet about three inches to his left. His own slug plunged into the man's vest, about an inch below his rib cage.

The man staggered, swinging his pistol around again. Not wanting the shooter to get off another shot and possibly hit one of the other diners, Stillman plugged him again, this time through the heart.

The man staggered back into another table, upsetting it, and fell amid a clatter of dishes and a volley of surprised yells from the crowd.

Stillman climbed quickly to his feet just as another man at the front of the room yelled, "You son of a bitch, Stillman!"

"Get down!" Stillman shouted to the room in general as the man extended a gun and fired. The slug sailed wild, shattering a bracket lamp. Raising his own Colt, Stillman squeezed off a round. The man had moved as Stillman fired, and ran into the lobby.

Cursing under his breath, Stillman zigzagged around tables and cowering diners, and ran into the lobby. Swinging right, he saw the second gunman mounting the stairs to the second-floor balcony.

"Hold it!" Stillman ordered.

The man turned and fired, his slug shattering a picture frame near Stillman's shoulder. Stillman's pistol barked, but the slug tore harmlessly into a railing post as the gunman topped the stairs.

Stillman took the steps two at a time. When he made the open second story, he turned to his left and saw the gunman running down the balcony. The lobby opened to his left, over a carved oak rail.

The man was about thirty feet beyond Stillman when a door opened and two burly men walked out of a room. Seeing the man running toward them with a gun in his hand, one of the burly gents, whom Stillman recognized as a stagecoach guard, yelled, "Hey, what's goin' on here?"

The gunman fired at him. Cursing, the guard and the

other gent ducked as the bullet plunked into the door frame. Red-faced with anger, the shotgun guard drew the hogleg from his hip and aimed at the gunman, who had stopped and was now tossing panicked glances between Stillman and the two gents impeding his escape.

Seeing Stillman in his firing line, the guard froze with his gun extended. "Ben, that you?"

Before Stillman could answer, the gunman swung toward the sheriff and squeezed off a round. Stillman dropped to a knee and watched as the gunman, glancing at the shotgun guard, who was still bearing down on him with his hogleg, ran to the railing. Hesitating for only a moment, he hurled himself over.

He landed in the lobby with a loud thud. A woman screamed and a man cursed.

Stillman bolted to the railing and looked down in time to see the gunman getting up. The man ran, limping, toward the double front doors.

Stillman bellowed, "Stop or you're wolf bait, amigo!" The man stopped and turned, swinging his pistol. Before he could shoot, Stillman shot him twice through the brisket. He fell into a potted plant and hit the floor with a groan.

Stillman turned to the stagecoach guard and the other gent. "Avery, you two all right?"

The two men were looking over the railing. "No holes in our hides, Ben. What the hell's goin' on?"

Without responding, Stillman hurried down the stairs. In the lobby, several people had gathered around the inert figure lying facedown on the floor.

The manager, Leonard Kyle, looked at Stillman.

"What's going on, Ben? Who are these fellas? Or who were they, I should say."

Stillman turned the gunman over with his right foot. He was dead, all right, his shirt bloody. Like the other man, he had dark hair and a broad nose, but he wasn't wearing a mustache. His clothes were considerably shabbier as well. He looked like a drover who'd only partially cleaned up for town.

"This one here's Duke Lonnigan," Stillman said. "And I

believe the other one in the dining room is his brother, Joe. Joe always was a natty dresser. I put him and Duke away about seven years ago, for bank robbery. It was a family affair. I had to kill their old man and younger brother. Joe and Duke promised they'd come after me when they got out of the cooler."

"Well, I reckon they got out, huh?" the coach guard said.

Stillman nodded. "I heard they were released from Deer Lodge a few weeks back."

"What a mess they made of my hotel," Kyle carped, gazing around.

"Sorry about this, Leonard."

"It wasn't your fault, Ben."

"Anyone hurt?"

"I don't think so."

Stillman thumbed sweat from his brow and holstered his .44. So much for a little peace and quiet. Maybe in his next life, he thought, glancing at one of the townies. "Ralph, will you get Doc Evans over here so we can haul these bodies off?"

"You got it, Ben," the man said, turning for the door.

Stillman walked into the dining room. Most of the lunch crowd was up and milling around with stricken looks on their faces. A couple of well-dressed men stood around the dead man, smoking and chatting in hushed tones.

Stillman inspected the body. Satisfied Joe Lonnigan was dead, he turned to look for Pettigrew. The writer seemed to have exited with the others. But then Stillman saw the man's valise on the floor.

He heard a grunt and a sigh. The sounds seemed to have come from under the table at which Stillman and Pettigrew had been sitting.

Stillman lifted the cloth and peered under the table. The writer was hunkered there, on his knees, his arms over his head.

"Pettigrew?" Stillman said.

The writer turned his sweat-beaded face to him. "Is . . . is it safe to come out?"

"It's safe," Stillman said, trying not to smile.

"Thank God," the writer exclaimed as he crawled out from under the table.

When he'd gained his feet, his knees noticeably quaking, he glanced at the dead man. His face bleached, and he staggered backward until Stillman grabbed his arm to steady him. With a deep inhalation, Pettigrew donned his derby, then picked up his valise.

"I think you might be right, Sheriff," he said, still a little breathless. "This project might not be right for me after all. I think I'll return to New York. . . ."

"And stick to fiction?"

Pettigrew nodded. "And stick to fiction."

He jerked his coat down, brushed crumbs off his arms, then wheeled and headed for the door. Watching him go, Stillman saw that the inside left leg of his broadcloth trousers appeared damp, and noticed that his shoe squeaked as he walked. He moved awkwardly, favoring that foot.

Stillman fingered his mustache as a smile tugged at his lips.

Pistol Pete had pissed his pants.

2

AROUND THREE O'CLOCK that afternoon, Stillman sat at a table in the Drovers Saloon with his deputy, Leon McMannigle. The two men usually had a beer together this time of the day, and they were usually joined by the town's doctor and undertaker, Clyde Evans. Today, however, Evans didn't show up until nearly three-thirty.

The stocky, red-haired man in a cheap three-piece suit and round spectacles pushed through the batwings and wasted no time in marching up to the bar and slapping the zinc with the palm of his hand. "Ready for maneuvers, Mr. Burk?"

The bartender, Elmer Burk, clicked his heels together and fashioned a mock salute. "Aye, aye, General."

"Assume battle formation."

"Battle formation assumed, General."

"Fire at will, Mr. Burk."

"Aye, aye, General. Firing at will." Bottle of Spanish brandy in hand, Burke filled a shot glass.

"You do that so well, Mr. Burk," Evans said, licking his lips, carefully lifting the shot glass, and throwing it back. He slammed the empty glass onto the zinc and wiped his red soup-strainer mustache with the back of his hand. "Let the barrage continue, Mr. Burk. The enemy is still at large."

"Aye, aye, sir," Burk said, refilling the shot glass.

Evans tipped the drink back, and stiffened as the liquor warmed his insides. He groaned with pleasure. "Ahhh . . ."

"Another volley, General?"

Evans squirmed around, working the kinks out of his broad boxer's shoulders. "One more volley, reinforced with the usual. Nasty devils need to be taught a lesson they won't forget. Then I'll retreat behind the pickets over there." Evans gestured at Stillman and McMannigle, who watched the routine with bemused smiles.

Burk filled another shot glass, and as Evans tipped it back, Burk filled a mug from his beer keg, scraped off the foam with a rake, and topped off the glass.

"You're a good man, Mr. Burk," Evans said as he dropped several coins on the bar. "Rest assured you'll be recommended for the highest of decorations. The highest in the land."

"Thank you, General." Burk saluted the doctor.

"You're welcome, Mr. Burk. At ease." Evans returned the salute, grabbed his beer, and sauntered, a trifle wobbly, to Stillman's table. He set his beer carefully down, slid out a chair, dropped his bowler on the chair beside him, and collapsed with a sigh.

"Tough day, Doc?" McMannigle asked.

Stillman's deputy was a handsome black man with a red cotton bib-front shirt, black vest, and flat-brimmed black Stetson. A former buffalo soldier, he lived in one of the town's three whorehouses and enjoyed the ministrations of the soiled doves, all of whom adored him, in return for keeping out the riffraff.

"Busy indeed, thanks to your boss here," Evans said, glancing at Stillman.

"Thanks to the two hombres who tried perforating my person," Stillman said. "The good ole Lonnigan boys."

McMannigle grimaced. "Boy, that was close, Ben. Sorry I wasn't there to back your play."

"You're not my bodyguard, Leon." Stillman sipped his

beer. "Anyway, it saved me from that Eastern writer."

Evans looked at Stillman darkly and shook his head. "I don't see how you do it—both of you. Living in the shadow of death constantly. And the more time you put in, the more men you put away, the more enemies you make, any of which could come after you—anywhere, anytime."

"You're starting to sound like that Eastern writer," Stillman quipped. "You missed your calling, Doc."

Pensive, Evans ignored the comment. " 'To give light to them that sit in darkness and in the shadow of death,' " he quoted, and sipped his beer. Smacking his lips, he said, "The Book of Luke, chapter one, verse seventy-nine."

" 'At the door of life, by the gate of breath,' " Stillman recited, " 'there are worse things waiting for man than death.' "

"Swinburne," Evans said with a thin, knowing smile. "Sheriff, you're a learned man."

"I married a schoolteacher," Stillman said with a shrug, lifting his glass.

"Or as Miss Jenny over at Mrs. Lee's place always says," Leon said, saluting with his beer mug, " 'Eat, drink, and couple like minks, for tomorrow you could come down with one hell of a pony drip, and Mrs. Lee will ban you from the premises.' "

Stillman and Evans laughed. They turned to the batwings as another man entered. He was a tall, slender man with light brown hair, wearing a string tie and what looked like a new, split-tail frock coat, cream Stetson pushed back on his freshly barbered head. His black boots were polished to a high gloss.

The man waved a greeting at the lawmen and Evans.

"Well, don't you look nice," Stillman said, friendly mockery in his tone. "Matt, I suspect there's a young lady waiting for you somewhere."

"She couldn't be over at the Anchor Ranch now, could she?" Leon asked, grinning around his cigar.

"Oh, I guess she could be," Matt Parrish said, not minding the good-natured harassment.

Friends with all these men, he'd been the owner/operator

of the Parrish Ranch since his father, the venerable Billy Parrish, died three years ago. Parrish's Circle P outfit was one of three large spreads in the Three-Witch Valley, southeast of Clantick, in the Two-Bear Mountains. "Even made a special trip to town to get me some duds," the young man said, spreading his hands to indicate his outfit. "How do I look?"

"Like a New Orleans pimp," said another man entering the saloon. There was no good-natured ribbing in the man's brusque tone.

Stillman watched as Vince Blacklaws swaggered up to the bar and ordered a double shot and a beer. Blacklaws's father owned the largest of the three spreads in Three-Witch Valley, the Copper Kettle. Vince was a tall, rangy cowboy in his late twenties, all hard angles and straight lines, with a belligerent face and flat, implacable eyes. A well-oiled Colt hung low on his dusty chaps.

Young Parrish watched the man with an angry flush on his face. Stillman knew there was no love lost between these two men, both born twenty-six years ago to competing ranch families in Three-Witch Valley. But then, no one cared much for the Blacklaws family. They had a reputation for being clannish and opportunistic. Stillman had always feared that Leonard Blacklaws, Vince's father, would try to run Parrish and Tom Suthern's outfit, Anchor Ranch, out of Three-Witch Valley by force, thus igniting a land war.

That hadn't happened, however. In fact, Blacklaws and the other two ranchers had seemed to arrive at an uneasy truce, realizing that the costs of a war would far outweigh any benefits. Still, that didn't keep Vince Blacklaws and Matt Parrish from going head-to-head now and then.

"You look downright civilized, Matt," Stillman said, hurrying to compliment young Parrish, trying to distract the rancher from Blacklaws's gibe. "Where'd you get that tie anyway? I should have one of those for Sundays."

"Yeah, you like it?" Parrish said, his attention successfully diverted from Blacklaws. Looking down at the tie, he said, "Over at Mr. Butler's place. He said he just got a shipment in from St. Louis."

"I'd say you look as spiffy as a royal wedding train," Doc Evans allowed. "I'd get me a tie like that, but what's the point? I don't go to church."

"I bet the Widow Kemmett wouldn't mind seeing you all spiffied up now and then," McMannigle said with a speculative air not lacking in amusement.

Doc Evans only chuffed and lifted his beer to his lips.

Parrish and Stillman smiled. Then Parrish said, "Well, I best get that beer I came for and hit the trail."

"See you, Matt," Stillman said.

"Say hi to Nancy," McMannigle said. Nancy Suthern, whose father owned the Anchor Ranch, which abutted Parrish's, was the girl Matt had been courting for nearly a year.

"I'll do that," Parrish said, turning toward the bar.

"Yeah, greet Nancy for me too," Vince Blacklaws said, dryly as, his back to the room, both elbows on the mahogany, he lifted his beer to his lips.

Stillman tensed as he watched Parrish. But the young rancher appeared in too good a mood to let Blacklaws rankle him. "Well, I'll do that, Vince. And I'm sure she'll appreciate that." Only a trace of sarcasm marred Parrish's affable tone.

He ordered a beer from Elmer Burk and sipped it quietly at the bar, a good ten feet to Vince Blacklaws's left. When it looked like no trouble would erupt between the two cow men, Leon McMannigle drained his beer and, setting the empty mug on the table, stood with a sigh. "Well, I better make my four o'clock rounds, I reckon. I'll see you tonight, eh, Doc? Remember, we got a blackjack game over at Mrs. Lee's place tonight. Eight o'clock."

"How could I forget?" Evans said. With a snide smirk, he turned to Stillman. "Your deputy might need a grubstake tomorrow, Ben, to keep him from starving to death."

"Don't count your chickens before they hatch, Doc." McMannigle donned his hat and turned for the door. "Your luck is bound to run out sooner or later."

Then he was gone, and Stillman and Evans settled into desultory conversation. The only other customers in the saloon, Parrish and Blacklaws, drank their beers in silence while Elmer Burk climbed a stool to polish the mirror behind the bar.

Stillman knew the peace was too good to last, however. He tensed when he saw Blacklaws half turn to Parrish. Blacklaws mumbled something Stillman couldn't hear, but it was obviously a goad or an insult. Parrish's neck reddened, but he only lowered his eyes and kept quiet.

Blacklaws had opened his mouth to say something else when Stillman broke in. "Hey, Vince, either keep your damn trap shut or get the hell out of here. Your choice."

Blacklaws turned to Stillman, indignant. "Well, pardon me all to hell, Sheriff, but I was just tryin' to make conversation with my neighbor is all. Just asked him if I was gonna get an invite to his weddin'."

"The day I'd invite you to my wedding, Vince, is the day hell freezes over and the devil's laid out in a block of ice."

Blacklaws looked at Stillman while raising a hand to indicate Parrish. "See there, Sheriff? Now, is that any way for a man to talk to his neighbor?"

"You've had your fun, Vince," Stillman said, his hard gaze drilling the blond Blacklaws. "Now finish your beer and get out of here."

"But—"

"Out!" Stillman yelled.

Blacklaws saw that the lawman was done fooling with him. "Whew!" he said, as though exasperated by the treatment. He tossed his beer back, slammed the empty mug on the bar. "When a man can't even enjoy a friendly conversation in his own town's saloon, the world is goin' to hell in a handbasket!" he exclaimed, marching haughtily through the batwings.

"Sorry, Ben," Parrish said. "I know I shouldn't let him get to me."

"No, you shouldn't," Stillman acknowledged. "The reason he pushes you, Matt, is because he knows you're an easy prod. He's bored—can't you see that?—and he's just boilin' for a fight to entertain himself."

"That boy's always been like that," the bartender, Elmer

Burk, said as he stared through the batwings. Turning to Parrish, he said, "I just wish if you're gonna fight, you'd do it outside. I don't need any more of my tables or windows broke."

"And I don't need your company over at the jailhouse either," Stillman added to the young rancher.

Parrish flushed, ashamed. "You won't have me over there anymore, Ben. I promise you that. I have a ranch to run, and I don't have time to fight with the likes of Vince Blacklaws. Sorry I let him get me riled. I've just had a lot on my mind lately."

"Nancy's father?" Doc Evans asked him.

Parrish turned full around now, and hooked his boot heel over the brass rail running along the base of the bar. "Yeah, I'm gonna make ole Tom Suthern another offer for his land tonight when I go over there for supper. He's been feelin' more poorly than usual, and Nancy thinks he might sell finally. I sure could use that land. I could run a whole other herd over there. And he's got the best water in the valley."

"I don't see why he wouldn't sell to you now that you and Nancy are fixing to get hitched," Stillman said. "With his arthritis and heart problems, I'd think Tom would be more than willing to part with all that work."

"I have a feelin' he'll come around," Parrish said. "At least, that's what Nancy thinks anyway."

"Well, don't get your hopes up too high," Evans counseled. "Ole Tom's a proud man. Even if you are marrying his daughter, he might see selling his land as the next-to-last step before selling out altogether, if you get my drift."

"I do," Parrish said with a nod. He donned his hat. "Well, I better get out there. Supper's always straight up at six at the Anchor." He smiled with irony. When he'd bidden Stillman, Evans, and Burk good evening, he left the saloon.

"What do you think?" Stillman asked Evans. "You've known old Tom Suthern longer than I have. Do you think he'll sell to Parrish?"

Evans shrugged and lit a brandy-soaked cigar. Blowing the thick, blue smoke, he said, "I reckon it depends on how bad Tom's ailing these days. I wouldn't know—he won't let me or any other sawbones within two miles of his place." Evans puffed more smoke, then removed the cigar and studied the coal. "And it also depends on how hard young Parrish pushes. Matt's had his own reputation for hotheadedness, you know, Ben. If he does anything to rile ole Tom, I'd say he's gonna be heading back to his own place with his tail between his legs."

Stillman thought about that as he stared out the window, where traffic moved slowly this late Saturday afternoon and the autumn shadows were lengthening. "I don't think that'll happen," he speculated. "Matt's matured quite a bit since I first met him. His old man's death and having to take on the ranch's operation has seen to that."

"I 'spect so," Evans said hopefully.

Such hope was rendered suspect when, as Stillman and Evans were leaving the saloon, a townie ran toward them, his face flushed with excitement.

"Sheriff, come quick!" the man yelled. "Parrish and Blacklaws are tanglin' like grizzlies over at the post office!"

3

"SHIT!" STILLMAN COMPLAINED. "Doc, you might as well come along in case there are any bones to set."

"I say let 'em fight it out, get it out of their systems once and for all."

"You're just tryin' to drum up more business," Stillman quipped as he stepped off the boardwalk, angling across First Street.

Grudgingly, Evans followed the lawman. "All right, I'll come," he said. "But I'm not helping you break up the fight. The last time I tried to break up a fight, the bastards broke my glasses."

"Don't worry—Leon's probably already there."

"Uh-uh," said the townie who'd summoned Stillman, shaking his head. The man was trotting along behind Evans. "McMannigle was called off by Mrs. Bjornson. Her niece's cat fell into that empty well pit they shoulda boarded up a long time ago, and he's tryin' to get it out."

"Well, then, I guess it's just you and me, Doc," Stillman said as he turned the corner and started down a side street.

He crossed the street and paused when he heard and saw the commotion outside the post office.

Parrish and Blacklaws were in the throes of battle. The postman, Ed Uhlich, stood nearby cajoling both men, to little effect. A few other townsmen, mostly shop workers, had formed a small crowd around the combatants, their expressions ranging from mild disgust to amusement. Both fighters had lost their hats, and their hair was wild, their faces flushed with fury.

Parrish ducked as Blacklaws threw a roundhouse.

Blacklaws's fist sailed wild, and Parrish punched his right kidney with a hard left jab. Blacklaws sprawled face-first against the brick post office, and Parrish was about to punch him again when Stillman mounted the boardwalk and grabbed him from behind, pinning his arms behind his back.

"Let me go, goddamnit, Ben! I've had enough of his insults and smart talk!"

"Simmer down now, Matt, or I swear I'm gonna throw you both in jail. Doc, grab him," he said as Blacklaws swung around toward Parrish.

Evans cursed and reluctantly shoved Blacklaws back against the office, bulling into the young firebrand's chest and pinning him there with a bear hug of sorts.

"I swear, Vince, you break my glasses, I'm gonna set your next fracture crooked!" the doctor warned.

"He started it, Sheriff," Blacklaws yelled. "He threw the first punch—didn't he, Ed?" he asked the postman.

Still holding Parrish's arms behind his back, Stillman turned to Uhlich, who looked vaguely reluctant. "He's right, Ben," the man said. "Matt here . . . he jumped on Vince like a roadrunner on a rattler. It started inside. I warned 'em both to get outside if they were gonna fight, and then there was hell to pave and no hot pitch."

"He was sayin' bad stuff about Nancy, Ben," Parrish said, struggling against Stillman's hold. "I told him if he didn't shut up, he was gonna be damned sorry. But he didn't shut up. He just kept goin', so . . ."

"All right, all right," Stillman said. "Now, Matt, I'm

gonna turn you loose. If you go after Blacklaws again, you're spending the night in jail. Understand?"

Parrish glared at Blacklaws, whom the stocky doctor still had pinned against the post office. Blacklaws glared back.

Stillman tightened his grip on Parrish's arms, shaking the young man. "Understand?" he repeated.

Parrish nodded. "I understand," he said. "But he better keep his distance from me, or all bets are off."

"Same goes for you, Vince," Stillman said. "Any more punches get thrown, you're going to jail."

"I hear you, Sheriff," Blacklaws said, acquiescing. "Remember, it wasn't me that started this thing."

Stillman released Parrish and told Evans to free Blacklaws. Parrish stooped to pick up his hat, trying to keep his heated eyes off his enemy, who was accepting his own Stetson from the postman.

"Ed, any damage inside?" Stillman asked.

The postman shook his head. "Nah, they took it outside before they started swingin', praise the Lord."

"What in the hell were you two doing here together?" Stillman asked the two fighters.

They looked cowed, but their nostrils still swelled, and their eyes flashed barely controlled rage.

"I came to pick up my mail like I always do when I come to town," Parrish explained.

"Me too," Blacklaws said, pulling a crumpled envelope from his back pocket, as if for proof. "I didn't know he was gonna be here, or I woulda stayed clear. I wasn't lookin' for no fight. I was just gonna pick up my mail and head on back to the ranch."

Parrish laughed caustically. "If you weren't lookin' for a fight, then why were you sayin' that stuff about Nancy?"

"That's enough, Matt," Stillman said. "Where's your horse?"

"Over at Auld's Livery."

"Mount and ride."

Parrish cast one more acrimonious gaze at his foe, then nodded. "All right, Ben," he said. Looking chagrined and brushing the dust off his new coat, he turned and walked toward First Street.

When he was gone, Stillman turned to Blacklaws. "As for you, Vince, I don't want you and Matt meeting up to continue this little barn dance on the trail somewhere."

"But Sheriff, I got chores to—"

"That's an order, Vince. You obey it or spend the night in the lockup. Which is it?"

Blacklaws sighed and licked the blood trickling from his cracked lower lip. His right eye was swelling. He looked considerably worse than Parrish, who hadn't appeared too beat up, although his new clothes would need a thorough dusting.

"All right, Sheriff," Blacklaws grumbled. He reached into his pocket, producing a wad of wrinkled greenbacks and some silver. "Looks like I might have just enough for an hour in one of the whorehouses. Guess I can at least make a time of it."

"There you go," Evans said, chuckling. The doctor, an infamous philanderer and frequenter of fallen women, fell silent when Stillman gave him a disapproving stare.

The sheriff turned his gaze to Blacklaws. "If any more fights break out between you and Parrish," Stillman warned, "you'll both go before the judge. I hope I've made myself clear."

Blacklaws nodded. "Very clear, Sheriff."

"Now get the hell out of my sight."

Blacklaws strolled off in his ambling, devil-may-care gait, and Stillman watched him.

Evans sidled up to the sheriff. "Think the fighting's over between those two?"

"In town it is," Stillman said with grim certainty. "I know that for a fact."

"Yeah, but what about in the country?" Evans said, thoughtfully chewing his mustache as he watched Blacklaws disappear down an alley.

Matt Parrish followed the trail south of Clantick, across the prairie that rose gradually to the first front of the Two-Bear

Mountains. The mountains were lovely this time of the year, mid-fall, with the foliage turning russet and brown and the aspens in the creases coloring the gold of morning sunlight.

But Parrish's thoughts were not on the mountains; they were on Vince Blacklaws and what Blacklaws had said in the post office about Nancy. Apparently, he'd seen Nancy swimming nude in Upper Three-Witch Creek one recent day, and instead of gigging his horse politely away, he'd sat on a spur over the creek, ogling her.

"Yeah, she looks all nice and sweet in those frilly dresses she always wears, but when you see her with her clothes off, why, that's one ripe wench!"

Parrish had dropped his mail and moved toward Blacklaws, fury blurring his vision and grinding his molars. Before he could take a swing, Ed Uhlich had jumped between him and Blacklaws and ordered them outside.

Now as Parrish rode his big paint mare, he realized he was grinding his molars again as he remembered Blacklaws's remarks, his lascivious gaze, and characteristically cocky demeanor.

"Son of a bitch, hawking Nancy like that . . ."

He wasn't sure if he should tell Nancy about Blacklaws watching her bathe. It might just upset her; she was a rather timid girl. But then again, Parrish didn't want her bathing out where Blacklaws could watch her either. His face warmed as another wave of anger washed over him, and he realized that what made him angriest was knowing that Blacklaws had seen more of Nancy's body than he, Parrish, had. And Parrish had been paying suit to her for over a year.

Parrish shook his head to ward away the incriminating thought. He was starting to think like Blacklaws now.

As he traversed a low pass and entered the foothills, he decided he wouldn't tell Nancy about Blacklaws. The information would only upset her, and the chances of Blacklaws riding near Upper Three-Witch Creek when Nancy was bathing again were minimal. Parrish knew that Nancy's outdoor baths were for fun and relaxation, and she indulged in them only when her ranch chores would allow.

Parrish looked down at his clothes. There were no tears, he saw, and for that he was grateful. The duds had cost him a small bundle, but he hadn't bought any new clothes in a couple years. Tonight he especially wanted to impress Nancy as well as her father. Not that a new wardrobe would convince old Tom Suthern to sell his ranch to his future son-in-law, but the old man would at least see that Parrish meant business.

When Parrish neared a brushy ridge an hour later, he reined his horse off the wagon trail and into a shallow ravine through which a tributary of Three-Witch Creek ran, tinkling over rocks. He tethered the horse to a willow, then walked over to the stream. He washed his face and combed his hair.

After inspecting his hat and brushing seeds and trail dust from the crown, he donned it, then climbed back onto the mare and resumed his course along the wagon road that climbed the ridge and dipped down into the Three-Witch Valley, so named after an ancient Gros Ventre legend about witches and the disappearance of various Indian travelers.

Fifteen minutes later, he approached a gate with a lodge-pole stretched over the top. Into each end of the lodgepole, an anchor had been burned. Parrish pushed through the gate and gigged his horse up the tree-shaded lane.

Soon a collection of log buildings and corrals revealed themselves in a clearing, and Parrish rode up to the two-story ranchhouse with a broad front veranda on which a spittoon and several wicker chairs sat. Parrish suppressed the urge to shake his head at the boards missing from the veranda's rotting floor, and the peeling paint on the clapboard-sided lodge.

A lovely girl with flaxen hair and wearing a simple but elegant cotton blouse and flowing purple skirt stepped through the lodge's front door, flashing even, white teeth between cherry-red lips.

"Well, hello there, stranger," Nancy said.

As she stopped under the awning, grinning up at him, Parrish ran his eyes down her hourglass figure with its high, firm bust. He had an image of her swimming naked, and knew a moment of both shame and arousal.

"Stranger?"

"I haven't seen you since last week, Mr. Parrish. When a girl doesn't see her young man for a week, she starts to wonder what's been keeping him so close to home. Do you have another girl stashed over there at the Circle P?" She crossed her arms over her breasts and regarded him with a capricious cast to her gaze.

Parrish laughed. "No, there's no other girl, Miss Suthern. I'll tell you what there is, though, and that's about a mile and a half of fence to stretch, a new well to dig, and over a hundred and fifty cattle to drive down from my summer pastures before the snow flies. That's what's been makin' me a stranger these days, I'm afraid."

"In that case, why don't you light a spell, you poor over-worked man. I was worried you'd forgotten about supper tonight."

"Oh, I never forget supper," Parrish said, dismounting. "There are many things I forget, but supper is not one of them. And neither are you." He approached her, took her hands in his, and kissed her gently on the lips.

When he pulled away, she gazed at him frowning. Lightly touching the bridge of his nose, she said, "What happened there?"

Parrish brought a finger to his nose and looked at the light blood smudge. "Oh, my horse head-butted me," he lied. No sense in worrying her over his scuffle with Vince Blacklaws. "Haven't trained her worth a darn, I reckon." Grinning and changing the subject, he said, "I'll run her over to the corral and be right back. I'm not late, am I?"

"As a matter of fact, you have twenty minutes to spare. When you return from the corral, you can join Dad in his den. I'll be in the kitchen."

"Sounds good."

"Matt," Nancy called.

Leading the mare away, Parrish turned back to Nancy.

She was adjusting the pin holding her flaxen hair in its lush bun. Renegade wisps danced about her long, creamy neck. Her eyes were vaguely troubled. "Are you going to talk to him about—you know?"

"What kind of mood's he in?"

"Well, he hasn't thrown any plates or kicked any dogs so far today."

"I'll give it a try then," Parrish said with a wistful grin.

When she didn't return the smile, he said, "I'm sorry, Nancy. I know how hard this is on you—watching your father get old. I remember how it was with my own dad and mom."

Nancy nodded. "He has to sell to you, Matt. He just has to. I can't leave him here alone. Tommy only comes home when he runs out of money. He's no help."

"We'll convince him eventually, you and me," Parrish said with a reassuring smile. "Don't worry."

She pursed her lips stoically and smiled. "I'm a Suthern. We Sutherns are tough as brass. That means, once we're married, you better mind your p's and q's, Mr. Parrish."

"Oh, boy," Parrish said with a chuckle, swinging around toward the barn. "What have I gotten myself into?"

"Nothing you can get out of now," Nancy called after him, her voice turning jovial once again.

Parrish unsaddled the paint mare and turned it into the corral off the main barn, nodding to a couple of the Anchor hands as he did, noting the stiff nods and grave gazes they returned. Most of the men were leery of him, he knew, because they knew he was after Anchor. A few had worked for old Tom Suthern a good many years, and ranch hands tended to be as loyal as they were resistant to change, not to mention suspicious of their neighbors. Most of the other men on Suthern's roll were hardcases who couldn't find jobs elsewhere. In his old age, Suthern had grown so cantankerous that he had to hire whoever would work for him.

On the way back to the house, Parrish saw Nancy's brother step off the front porch and turn toward Parrish. Tom Jr. was a lanky kid of nineteen, two years younger than his sister. The hair hanging off his collar was a shade darker than his sister's. He wore a narrow-brimmed Stetson, a black duster, and a black gunbelt trimmed with silver conchos. His double-hung *buscadero* holsters held matching, ivory-handled Colts.

The getup told Parrish the kid had read too many Ned Buntline stories about the Wild West.

"Evenin', Tommy," Parrish said.

The kid only nodded, barely looking at Parrish as he passed.

Parrish paused and called after him, "Not dining with us tonight?"

"Nah, I got places to go and people to see," young Parrish said without turning around. Then he stopped and turned to face Parrish. "Don't fool yourself about my old man selling out to you, Matt," he said with a sneer, revealing a chipped front tooth. "No way it's gonna happen. Not as long as I'm around anyway."

"When are you ever around, Tommy?" Parrish couldn't help gibing.

"I'm around enough to know this place will be mine when the old man's pushin' up daisies."

"I don't think that's true, Tommy," Parrish said, referring to the well-known fact that the kid had been written out of Tom Suthern's will the day he'd held up a stage a few miles outside of Clantick. The judge had given him probation when he'd turned in the three accomplices who'd gotten away, but old Tom didn't believe in probation. In light of the fact that the holdup was only one in a string of his son's transgressions, the old man had written him out of his will, the news of which had spread like wildfire. Old Tom had said that as long as he was alive it was his duty as the malcontent's father to offer him food and shelter, but the Anchor and all its land and cattle would go to Nancy.

"It's true enough," the kid said. Then his eyes grew dark and the lines in his young face planed out. "Unless you're callin' me a liar, Parrish."

Nonchalantly, the kid slid his duster behind the gun on his right hip, revealing the ivory grips. He watched Parrish expectantly, but with too much melodrama for Parrish to take him seriously.

Parrish knew better than to laugh, however much he

wanted to. That could set the kid off, and Parrish would have to kill Nancy's brother. Instead, he said, "Tommy, you're gonna get yourself drilled one of these days."

"Am I? By who? You?"

Before Parrish could answer, Nancy called from the house, "Matt, Dad's waiting for you in the den."

"Sorry, Nancy," Parrish said, only half turning and keeping one eye on her surly brother who fancied himself the next Black Bart.

The kid gave another sneer, then cursed under his breath and headed for the corral.

Turning away from the cub, Parrish headed for the lair of the old lion himself.

4

PARRISH WAS TURNING a hall corner in the Suthern house when a loud thump shook the floor. Breaking into a run, he entered Tom Suthern's study.

"For heaven's sake, Mr. Suthern!" he exclaimed, hurrying over to where the old man had fallen in the corner between the liquor cabinet and the wall, an overturned chair on his legs. "What happened?"

His question was echoed by Nancy, running into the room, wide-eyed with worry. "Dad, what on earth did you do?"

Suthern's broad, leathery face was red with exertion, and his leonine mane of white hair, which made his head seem too big for his emaciated body, was mussed about his forehead. He winced with pain and frustration.

"I was . . . I was trying to reset the clock above the liquor cabinet, and the damn chair fell out from under me," he said through several ragged grunts.

Nancy crouched beside her father and regarded the old man nervously. "Are you okay? Did you break anything? Do you—?"

"No, I didn't break anything, damnit," old Suthern

growled. "I ain't made of glass, you know. The damn chair just fell out from under me, that's all." He lifted his arms. "Well, don't just stand there gawkin' at me, for chrissakes. Give me a hand up!"

"You got it, Mr. Suthern," Parrish said as he and Nancy each took an arm and gently heaved the frail man to his feet.

"There you go, Dad," Nancy said, watching her father's face for more signs of pain. "How do you feel?"

"Like I always feel," Suthern said, taking a deep breath as he shifted his scowling, washed-out eyes around the room. "Stiff and sore and mad as hell."

"Oh, Dad," Nancy said. "What a worry you are. Don't you know you shouldn't be standing around on chairs?" She was brushing lint and dust off his corduroy jacket and his cream shirt with its buttoned collar.

"Now, don't go patronizin' me, damnit, girl!" Suthern said, shrugging her off. "I wasn't standin' around on that chair for the thrill, ye know. I was tryin' to set that damn clock. I told Tommy to do it way last week, but you s'pose he ever got around to it?"

"You might have asked me," Nancy pointed out as she righted the overturned chair.

"You know I don't like women in my study." Suthern ambled to a sofa angled before his acre-sized, leather-covered desk behind which a battered hide rocker sat. He turned his back to the sofa and not so much sat as collapsed with a deep sigh, throwing his head back. "Women always feel they have to fool with something, then I can't find it again."

"It's called cleaning, Dad," Nancy said with a tolerant, complicitous glance at Parrish. "If you don't let me dust in here again soon, this place is going to look like the Mohave Desert."

"Sounds like her mother," Suthern told Parrish. "Cleanliness is next to godliness and all that rot. Pour me a drink, will you, Matt?"

Nancy started to speak, but the old man cut her off with an angry wave of his gnarled hand. "And don't tell me I can't have a glass of brandy, for chrissakes!"

"I wasn't," Nancy said, fashioning another patient smile. "I was just going to tell you not to overindulge. It makes you cross." She gave Parrish another ironic glance, then turned toward the door. "Supper will be soon, gentlemen," she called over her shoulder, and left.

Parrish poured brandy from the decanter on Suthern's desk, and gave the glass to the old man, who took a big, thirsty swallow. "Ah," he said, smacking his lips. "That's better. Pour yourself one, Matt."

"Don't mind if I do," Parrish said. "Just came from town. It's quite a ride."

"Cut the trail dust."

"If you say so," Parrish said, pouring a glass for himself. He took one of the two stuffed chairs beside the sofa, extended his legs, crossed his ankles, and sipped the brandy. Suthern may have been half-broke, but he still found credit for the best booze in the Territory.

Suthern blew his nose into a red handkerchief. "What were you doing in town, Matt?"

"Buying these," Parrish said, indicating his new clothes and the hat he'd tossed on the desk when he'd rushed into the study. "What do you think?"

Suthern squinted at Parrish's attire and nodded, thoughtful. "What's the occasion?"

"I hadn't bought any new duds in a while, so I figured as long as I was coming over here tonight, why not? Besides, I've needed a church jacket and tie for quite some time."

"You didn't buy that getup to impress me, I hope," Suthern grumbled, scowling at Parrish, his liquid blue eyes dubious. "New duds ain't gonna convince me to sell my spread to you, Matt, if that's what you're doin' here tonight."

Parrish maintained a neutral expression. "What makes you think that's what I'm doing here tonight?" He wondered if Nancy had told the old man, to prepare him. She might have been worried the old man would hit the ceiling and throw him out when Parrish made his offer.

"Just a feelin' I got," Suthern said. "I've always had the ability to tell the future, you know that?"

"You and my old man," Parrish said with an edgy half smile.

Suthern chuckled. "Yeah, old Billy—he claimed the same thing." He chuckled again, and shook his head. "I remember when he got a notion those Swedes nesting at the base of Long John Butte were collarin' beef from both our herds. We rode out there for a look-see, and sure enough, we caught several old boys with runnin' irons and three butchered carcasses. . . ."

"But the culprits weren't the Swedes," Parrish went on, finishing the old story as he smiled down at his brandy snifter. "They were the Eye-talians from Eagle Creek."

Suthern slapped his thigh, guffawing. "Can you imagine those damn dagos pullin' a stunt like that? I didn't even know they could ride!"

He laughed. Parrish smiled. "Whatever happened to them?"

"Went back overseas, I reckon. Couldn't stand the cold. One of the women stayed with a Josephson boy over by Baldy Butte. I heard she died giving birth to her third baby."

"That's right," Parrish said, nodding as he remembered.

"So that ain't what you're doin' here?" Suthern asked, his mood changing abruptly, his cold blue eyes on Parrish again.

Caught off guard, Parrish looked at him. "Come again?"

"You heard me."

Parrish fiddled with his drink. He couldn't very well lie to the man. Before he could say anything, Suthern said, "Goddamnit, Matt! That *is* what you're doin' here!"

"Let's let it go until after supper, Mr. Suthern."

Suthern's voice boomed as he jutted his choleric face at Parrish. "Let's let it go, period. I've told you twice now, I'm not sellin' out. As long as I'm still kickin', I'll own and operate Anchor. And I don't appreciate you taking advantage of your relationship with my daughter to push me off my place."

Parrish tried to squeeze a word in, but Suthern wouldn't have it.

"What do you want me to do? Move to town and live in one of them boardinghouses? Pshaw! You'll never find Tom Suthern livin' like some old bull at Mrs. Nelson's place, livin' in a closet and sittin' out on the veranda with the old crows who complain about their ailments and concoct big windies about their glory days. Pshaw! No matter how well you've hornswoggled my daughter into believing that's what I should do. Never!"

"I don't expect you to move to town and live with strangers, Mr. Suthern," Parrish said reasonably, wishing against wish that this conversation could have waited until after supper. The bull was out of the chute now, though. He might as well run with it. "I fully intend for you to move in with me and Nancy over at the Circle P, once we're married. We'll take care of you. You'll be just as comfortable there as you are here."

"I could never be comfortable away from Anchor! No, sir, I won't do it, Matt. You'll have to wait till after I'm dead to take Anchor. I won't have you pickin' my bones while I'm still alive."

Parrish looked at the old man indignantly. "I'm not pickin' your bones, Mr. Suthern, and I resent you sayin' I am. I'm simply trying to do what's best for all of us, your daughter included. You're half-broke and you're running this place into the ground. Good men won't work for you anymore, and those that are left hardly work at all. They're a bunch of misfits!"

Parrish heard his voice rising, but he couldn't control himself. "Why, half your fences are down, your cattle are mingling with mine and Blacklaws', and your creeks are bein' muddied something awful 'cause your men aren't keeping up with your herds."

Suthern stared at him, nostrils flaring.

Parrish continued. "Hell, look at this house! How long's it been since you've had it painted? And that windmill in the yard squawks louder every time I visit."

"Well, maybe you should stop visiting then!"

"Think about your daughter, Mr. Suthern. Nancy's going to worry something fierce about you after we're married and you're here all by yourself."

"I'm a cow man from my boot heels up," Suthern raged. "I settled this land alone, I'll leave it alone!"

His fierce, red eyes locked on something behind Parrish, and softened slightly. Parrish turned to see Nancy standing in the doorway. He wasn't sure how long she'd been there, but he figured the whole argument could have been heard in every room in the lodge—probably out in the bunkhouse even.

"I thought we were going to wait until after supper," she said quietly to Parrish.

Frustrated and angry at the old man, Parrish hemmed and hawed and finally shook his head. "I'm sorry, Nancy. He just won't listen to reason. He's more stubborn than a cow with a sucking calf!"

Suthern jerked his old lion's head at Parrish again. While he was just as fierce as before, his voice was low, the flinty words spat from puckered lips. "And you're nothin' but a goddamn opportunist, taking advantage of an old man's failin' health. Shame on you, Matt Parrish. What would your old man say about this?"

"Leave my old man out of this," Parrish said. He climbed to his feet, slammed his half-finished drink on the desk, and grabbed his hat. Turning to Nancy, he said, "I'm sorry, but I can't eat in the same house with this old bastard. I'm leavin'."

"Oh, Matt," Nancy said, wrinkling her eyes with consternation. "Won't you please stay? Dad wants you to stay, don't you, Dad?"

"No, I don't!" Suthern yelled from the sofa. "I want him outta here, an' I don't want to see his flea-bit hide ever again. And if you marry him, daughter, I'm gonna write you out of my will just like I did your worthless brother!"

Beside Nancy, Parrish turned and gaped at old Suthern. He looked at Nancy, whose face was white, her eyes wide with hurt.

"There's just no reasoning with that long-headed mule," Parrish said. "I'm sorry, Nancy."

He turned and walked to the front door, Nancy following on his heels. As he descended the porch, Nancy called to him, and he stopped and turned around.

"He doesn't know what he's saying, Matt," she said, wringing her hands and canting her head sympathetically at Parrish. "He's just mad at the world and mad at himself for getting old. Tomorrow he's going to be sorry for what he said. In a few days, I think he's going to be sorry for turning down your offer too, Matt. I just know he is."

"Well, I've done all I can," Parrish said with a deep sigh of frustration. He walked back onto the porch and kissed her cheek. "I'm sorry about the argument. You going to be all right?"

"Only if you ride back and see me tomorrow. I'm going to be worried about us tonight. I'm going to worry he's scared you off, and I don't know what I'd do if that happened."

"No need to worry about that," Parrish assured her, flashing a smile and squeezing her hands in his. "I love you, Nancy, and by God, I'm going to marry you."

"I love you too, Matt Parrish."

"Sorry we ruined your supper. I hate to see all that good food go to waste."

"I'll fix you and me a picnic lunch tomorrow. How does that sound?"

"That sounds nice." He smiled again and kissed her cheek. "You sure you're going to be all right?"

She nodded. "I'll be fine."

"Good night then."

"Good night, Matt," she said, and watched as he turned toward the corral.

Parrish was so shaken from his argument with Suthern that it took him a good fifteen minutes to get his horse properly bridled and saddled. When he finally mounted outside the main barn, he saw Suthern's assistant foreman, a hard-edged Mexican named Otero, watching him from the door of the blacksmith shop across the yard. The man's pistols winked in the fading light and the brim of his black hat shaded his hawklike features. Behind him, the clang of a hammer on an anvil rang out in the quiet, dusky air.

When Parrish gave an angry wave, Otero just stood there, staring. Parrish kneed his horse into a canter across the yard, and headed down the cottonwood-lined lane, hearing the mourning doves and meadowlarks and finding himself wishing the old man would die in his sleep tonight.

He'd just turned onto the main road and was heading west when two shots rang out to his right. His horse's ears twitched warily as Parrish reined the mare to a halt, listening.

The shots could have been one of the cowboys target-shooting, but Parrish didn't think so. There would have been more than two shots.

Finally, the rancher steered the mare off the trail and into the trees along the creek that angled around the main house. A few minutes later, he reined the horse to a sudden halt, casting his puzzled gaze at something lying on the footpath in the weeds across the creek.

A man.

Hurriedly, Parrish jumped off the mare, tied the horse to a tree, and scrambled across the shallow creek bubbling over rocks. As he knelt down, he saw the gray hair and coat, and his heart did a somersault.

Then he turned old Suthern over, saw the blood on his chest and neck, and froze with disbelief.

Someone had murdered Tom Suthern, who must have taken a walk out here after Parrish had left, to let off steam.

Jerking his head up and looking around, Parrish drew his Colt.

Just then a Spanish-accented voice called from the trees behind him, "Mr. Suthern!"

Parrish turned to see the Mexican, Otero, staring at him from about fifty yards away. Parrish remained squatting there for several seconds, not sure what to do, his heart tattooing his breast bone. Finally, Otero drew one of his guns and aimed at Parish.

"Hold it there, you murdering bastard!"

5

OTERO BEGAN RUNNING toward Parrish, who glanced at Suthern's inert body, then at the Colt in his hand.

Knowing how the scene must look and not taking the time to think beyond it, as Otero squeezed off a shot, Parrish bounded to his feet and splashed across the creek. Otero fired again, the slug slicing the air an inch off Parrish's right ear and making his paint mare whinny and pull at its reins.

"Easy, easy," the rancher urged the horse as, moving fast, he grabbed the reins from the tree and jumped onto the saddle.

Another shot rang out, and Parrish felt the burn of a bullet crease his left arm, just above the elbow. Turning, he saw Otero standing in the creek, gun raised.

"I didn't do it!" Parrish yelled.

Otero's revolver barked, the bullet clipping a tree branch a foot shy of Parrish's head.

"Goddamnit!" Parrish protested as, hearing the yells of more men approaching across the creek, he reined the mare toward the road and spurred it hard, plunging through brush and low branches.

"You murdering bastard!" Otero shouted behind him. To someone else, Otero yelled in his accented English, "Parrish killed the boss! He shot Mr. Suthern!"

Then the voices behind Parrish mingled inaudibly and diminished in volume until, by the time Parrish made the road, they were barely discernible above the sound of the birds and the rustle of the breeze in the brush.

Parrish halted the mare on the road, his heart fairly leaping in his chest, his hands and legs trembling with excitement, his head swirling. Taking a moment to gather his thoughts, he couldn't quite believe what they told him: Old Tom Suthern was dead.

Shot.

Murdered.

Otero believed that Parrish had done the killing, and now he probably had the other Anchor men believing the same thing. Parrish couldn't really blame them. The scene with him standing over the old man's dead body, a revolver in his hand, couldn't have looked more incriminating. What's more, the argument between Parrish and Suthern had probably been heard as far as the bunkhouse, for the study windows had been open to the freshening evening breeze.

Parrish looked toward the main lodge, which he couldn't see from this far away, wondering what to do. He felt a nearly overwhelming urge to ride back to the house and tell Nancy what had happened and assure her that he was not her father's killer.

He knew she would believe him. The only problem was, the Anchor men would probably kill him on sight and ask questions later. Virtually the whole crew were gun-handy firebrands. Parrish doubted the foreman, Charlie Klosterman, who had worked for Suthern for over ten years and whom Parrish knew and respected, could hold them at bay.

No, as much as he wanted to be with Nancy right now, to comfort her during this tragedy as well as to explain himself, riding back to the house would be his death sentence. He had to ride out of here, let the fires cool, and explain himself later.

That decided, he turned the mare around, and headed west down the road at a ground-eating gallop. The Anchor riders were no doubt heading back to the corral for their horses. They'd be on Parrish's trail in minutes.

The rancher had to get as much distance between him and them as possible. Last he'd heard, Suthern had eight men working for him—if you could call it working. Mostly they played cards and caroused. Some rode the owlhoot trail with Tommy Jr. Several were seasoned hardcases, good with their guns. Parrish didn't want them catching up to him out here, where he'd have to fight them alone. Against that eight, he wouldn't have a chance.

If he could make it home, he could hail his own six waddies from the bunkhouse, and hold off the Anchor crew while sending one of his own men for Sheriff Stillman in Clantick. Stillman and McMannigle would sort through this mess and realize that Parrish was innocent.

Those plans working through his mind, Parrish hunkered low in the saddle as the mare ate up the trail, which curved along Three-Witch Creek and traversed several lesser streams. The sun set, an orange ball plunging into the darkly humping shapes of the western Two-Bears. Shadows flooded the valley, angling down from the aspen pockets on the mountain slopes and engulfing the thick brome, bluestem, and buffalo grass that grew lush and golden along the bottoms.

Deer grazed in the parks near the creek, their coats cherry tan in the last light. Hearing the thuds of the mare's hooves, they bounded for the pine-timbered ridges or the cottonwood-choked draws.

The air cooled, drying the sweat on Parrish's face. Night birds shrieked and flicked their shadows over the darkening earth.

When he'd ridden for a half hour, Parrish took the left fork in the trail. Cresting a low divide, he reined the sweat-lathered mare to a sudden halt and squinted his eyes above and to his left.

Small, dark shapes spilled down from a timbered mountain peak. Parrish hoped it was deer. But then the last salmon light flashed on a spur or a rifle, and he knew it was the Anchor men. They'd taken a shortcut over the mountains, intending to cut him off on his way. home.

Damn. They had to want him even worse than he'd thought to negotiate that rugged route at twilight.

He scowled, pondering, then reined the mare back the way he had come, hoping the Anchor men hadn't seen him on the divide. When he came to the fork, he took the other tine, which led straight west, galloping the mare for a mile or so, then slowing her down to a walk, giving her a rest. Going where Parrish had decided to go, she'd have a steep climb in a few minutes.

It was true dark by the time Parrish had ridden over the saddle between Indian-Head Butte and Davis Mountain and followed White-Tail Creek until the lights of a small ranch shone before him, on the other side of the water murmuring above the solemn cries of coyotes and the occasional hoot of an owl.

Parrish kneed the mare down the shallow ravine, splashed across the creek, and jogged up the opposite bank. A minute later he was passing through the gate of the Harmon ranch, setting several cows in the paddock behind the barn to lowing. From the log cabin's front porch, a dog barked.

"Don't shoot, Jody," Parrish called, knowing his presence had been registered within the cabin and that his life-long buddy, Jody Harmon, was probably reaching for a Winchester. "It's me—Matt Parrish."

The door opened as Parrish reined up to the hitch rack before the stoop. A young man's slender silhouette appeared in the doorway, a lantern-lit kitchen behind him. He was holding a carbine down low at his side.

"Matt?" Jody Harmon called as he peered into the darkness. "What in the hell are you doing this far from home this time of the night?"

Parrish was whipped from the hard ride and his anxiety

over Tom Suthern's death. "I got trouble, Jody. Can I come in?"

"You bet," Jody said. He turned slightly and gestured at the kitchen with his rifle barrel. "Light and sit a spell."

Parrish climbed heavily out of the saddle and looped the reins over the hitch rack. As he climbed the stoop, Jody stepped to the side of the door and studied Parrish soberly. Usually when they were together, it was a time of joking and good-natured jeers. Both having grown up in the Two-Bear Mountains, their ranches about ten rugged miles apart, they'd known each other all their lives, and had spent many an hour together on roundup and around branding fires. Jody could tell from the steaming mare and Parrish's wrung-out appearance that this was no time for revelry, however.

Parrish doffed his hat and entered the cabin. Jody's wife, Crystal, was rocking their baby before the large fieldstone hearth in which a bright fire popped against the night's autumn chill. Crystal was a pretty, tomboyish blonde with bright, affably ironic eyes, clad in a flannel shirt and baggy duck trousers. The one-year-old snuggled against her shoulder wearing a knit nightcap and moccasins Crystal had no doubt sewn herself.

"Well, hello there, Mr. Parrish," Crystal said, characteristically buoyant. "Haven't seen you in a while. To what do we owe the honor?"

"Sorry to barge in on you so late, Crystal," Parrish said. Jody came in behind him, and Parrish turned to him quickly. "I just want you to know right off, Jody, I made sure I wasn't followed before I headed over the divide."

Jody glanced at his wife, then returned his puzzled gaze to Parrish. "What? Who'd be following you, Matt? What's going on?"

Parrish looked at Crystal, hesitating. Crystal settled the sleeping baby in the crib positioned near the fire, and walked into the kitchen. Reaching into a cupboard above the icebox, she said, "Have a seat, Matt. I don't usually offer liquor to my company on account of what the bottle did to my pa, but you look like a stiff shot would do you nothing but good."

She set a stone coffee mug on the table, splashed whiskey into it, then corked the bottle and set it nearby. Indicating a chair, she said with an impatient air, "Sit down, sit down."

"Thanks, Crystal," Parrish said, dropping his hat on the table and taking a chair. "I reckon I could use that drink."

He placed both hands around the cup, as though afraid he couldn't steady it with only one, and drank. With a sigh, he set the mug back on the table, leaving his hands around it, and looked at Jody, who'd taken a seat across from him.

Crystal stood near Jody, watching Parrish with her arms folded across her man's flannel shirt. At first, Parrish had been reluctant to speak in front of her, but then he remembered her toughness—she'd been born and raised in these mountains, just like Parrish and Jody—and was as hardy as or hardier than most seasoned waddies Parrish had known.

"Ole Tom Suthern is dead."

Jody stared at him, then asked quietly, "What happened?"

Parrish told the whole story, from his arrival at the Suthern ranch, through the shots he'd heard and his discovery of Suthern's body, to the Anchor riders cutting off his route home.

"I'm sure they didn't follow me," Parrish assured Jody and Crystal again. "It would've been nigh impossible at night anyway."

Crystal only nodded, lost in thought. Halfway through Parrish's story, she'd slumped into the rawhide chair at the end of the table, one leg curled beneath her, arms still folded across her shirt.

Jody saw Parrish staring at the bottle, and poured his friend another drink. "We have to get Ben Stillman out here," Jody said.

Parrish sipped the drink and said grimly, "He's gonna think I did it."

"No, he's not," Crystal was quick to reply. "Ben knows

you, Matt. He knows you wouldn't kill Tom Suthern or anyone else."

Uncertain of this, Parrish stared at the whiskey in his cup.

"You have any idea who shot him?" Jody asked.

"None."

"You didn't see anyone else around?"

Parrish shook his head. "Of course, ole Tom has made lots of enemies over the years, and since his arthritis turned worse he's been nastier than a bull buffalo with an itch he can't scratch."

"Think it could've been one of his men?" Crystal asked.

"That's what I figure," Parrish said. "One of 'em that was holdin' a grudge against ole Tom might've heard us arguing in the study and decided to take advantage of the situation. After the argument we had, who wouldn't think I shot him?"

Jody ran his hands through his straight, black hair, which betrayed his half-Indian heritage. His mother had been a Cree, his father an old mountain man and Ben Stillman's best friend.

"Ben will find out who did it," Jody assured Parrish.

Parrish shook his head, wincing doubtfully. "That's what I thought at first. I don't know, Jody. It looks bad. My mind's been over it, and it looks plain bad."

"There's nothing else to do," Crystal said. "You can't run, Matt. That would only make you look guiltier. Besides, if anyone can find who really did it, it's Ben. Jody'll ride to town for him tomorrow morning."

"You better go, Crystal," Jody said. "If the Anchor men come, I want to be here."

Crystal thought about it. "You'll tend the baby?"

Jody nodded.

"Well, don't you two teach little William Ben any cuss words while I'm gone," she said, trying to lighten the mood.

Jody smiled, but Parrish did not. He stared thoughtfully at the table, anxiously picking a callus on the palm of his right hand.

6

"LET'S MAKE A baby."

The words, spoken in a husky woman's voice, reached Stillman at the bottom of a deep doze. He opened his eyes to find his young wife, Fay, snuggling against his chest, kissing him gently.

"What'd you say?" he asked, looking at her and blinking sleep from his eyes. Pale dawn light filtered through the shade over the bedroom window.

"Let's make a baby."

"Now?"

"Why not? You're awake, aren't you? We're both ready for a child, aren't we?"

Stillman thought about it. Yes, he was ready for a child. He'd been reluctant when Fay had first brought up the idea several months ago. His job as a lawman was a risky one, and he recoiled at the possibility of his leaving a child fatherless. But after thinking about it, he had decided that he had no right to refuse Fay a child. She'd been wanting one so badly ever since Jody and Crystal had brought their little William Ben into the world last winter. No, he had no right to refuse her. Besides, as she had pointed out, in the event of his death, having his child to raise would be a great comfort to her.

She lifted her chin to look up at him with her French-dark eyes set like jewels in her elegantly beautiful face framed by thick, chocolate hair. She smiled tenderly. "Having second thoughts?"

"No, not really," Stillman said. "It's just a pretty big step."

"Oh, come on," Fay cajoled him, teasing, moving her hands to him beneath the sheets. "It's not such a big step if we take it together."

As her hands awakened his desire, he decided that, in his mid-forties, he wasn't getting any younger. At twenty-eight, Fay still had time, but what was the point in waiting any longer?

"There now—does that help you decide, Sheriff?" Fay said breathily in his ear as her masterful hands worked their bewitching magic beneath the sheets.

Stillman swallowed. "Yeah, it . . . certainly does."

"I can tell," Fay said with a husky chuckle.

She sat up and, facing him, lifted her nightgown over her head. He watched her hair cascade down her shoulders and around her lovely, pale, pink-nippled breasts. He leaned forward to kiss each in turn, hearing her coo softly with desire as she ran her hands through his hair.

He pulled her down to him, crawled gently atop her, and smiled into her face, her slitted eyes reflecting the brightening dawn light in the window. "I love you, Fay."

"Show me," she whispered, wrapping her arms around his neck and closing her mouth over his as she entangled her long, coltish legs around his back.

Later, after they'd eaten a quiet breakfast together in their kitchen, Stillman retrieved his gunbelt off a peg by the back door and notched it around his waist. "Well, what do you think?" he asked Fay, who was still sitting at the kitchen table, grading her students' papers while sipping coffee. "Did it work?"

Fay lifted her head to gaze at him, then brought her coffee cup to her lips. Speaking over its steaming rim, she said coquettishly, "What on earth are you talking about, Ben Stillman?"

"You know what I'm talkin' about," Stillman said. "You think we have a bun in the oven?"

Fay smiled. "Well, I don't know. These things take time. I think, just to be sure, though, we should turn in early tonight." She got up from her chair and moved to him, wrapped her arms around his neck. "Very early."

Stillman pulled her to him and kissed her, long and deep, feeling the swell of her bosom against his chest, feeling his desire grow once more. "I'm all for that," he said.

She looked at him seriously. "Really, Ben? You're not just doing it for me?"

He shook his head. "No. I was reluctant at first—you know that. But after I thought about it, I can't imagine not giving you a child, Fay. Hell, a woman with your brains and beauty not bringing a baby into this world would be a crying shame."

He kissed her again. She rested her head against his broad chest, kneading his heavy, rounded shoulders with her hands. "Oh, Ben—we're going to make a wonderful baby."

"I just hope it takes more after you than me," Stillman said with a smile. "Otherwise, the joke's gonna be on you."

He pinched her chin, and she laughed. He kissed her again. "I better get over to the office. It's almost eight. I'll see you tonight."

"I can't wait. You have a safe day, Mr. Stillman."

"Give those students hell, Mrs. Stillman," he said, grabbing his hat off its peg and opening the back door.

On the back stoop, Stillman studied the morning—breezy and cool with a few low-lying, dark-blue clouds over the buggy shed he'd converted into a horse stall and chicken coop. But the sun was peeking through, and Stillman suspected the sky would clear by noon, and they'd have a nice Indian summer before the first snowstorm of the season.

A rooster crowed from the chicken coop. "Coming,

Buster," Stillman hailed the chicken, heading across the yard.

When he'd fed and watered his chickens, he saddled his barrel-chested, long-legged bay, Sweets, and headed for the sheriff's office on First Street. He'd no sooner gotten a fire laid in the office's potbelly stove when he glimpsed movement out the window, and heard a horse whinny and stamp.

Frowning, he opened the door just as Crystal Harmon dismounted a steel-dust mare. The young woman was dressed for riding in jeans, cotton shirt, and duck coat, her Stetson snugged down low on her head. She was also wearing a pistol, Stillman saw. Her cheeks were pink from the cold forty-five-minute ride.

"Crystal, what in the dickens are you doing in town so early? Nothing wrong with Jody or little Bill, is there?"

Crystal shook her head as she mounted the short strip of boardwalk under the awning stretching the width of the small log sheriff's office. Stillman stepped aside to let her in out of the cold. "No, they're fine, Ben. It's Matt Parrish I'm here about."

"Oh, no," Stillman said, shutting the door behind him. "Don't tell me him and Vince Blacklaws got into it again."

"No, that's not it. I take it no one from the Anchor Ranch has told you the news?"

Stillman frowned and hooked his thumbs inside his shell belt. "What news is that?" Before she could reply, he held up his hands, stopping her, and said, "Wait. You look chilled." He moved a Windsor chair to the stove. "There you go—sit right there. Now tell me what's going on while I put some coffee on."

"Thanks." Crystal sat down, removed her hat and gloves, and tossed them on the floor to warm from the heat the ticking stove was just now starting to radiate. Rubbing her chilled hands together, she said, "Someone killed old Tom Suthern last night, Ben."

Stillman was at a cabinet, scooping coffee into an old tin coffeepot. He stopped and turned to her. "Oh, no."

Crystal nodded. "Apparently, the Anchor men think Matt did it."

Stillman's brows puckered as he slid his eyes from Crystal to stare darkly at the coffeepot. "I had a feeling you were going to say that."

"You did? Why?"

Stillman shook his head and resumed scooping coffee into the pot. When he'd filled it with water from the tin pitcher on the cabinet, he set the pot on the stove, moved to his desk, and cocked a hip on a corner, regarding Crystal gravely. "Tell me the whole story," he said. "Everything you know."

When she was finished, Stillman rubbed his jaw and gave a ragged sigh. Crystal watched him worriedly. "You don't think Matt actually did the killing, do you, Ben?"

Stillman looked at her. "Do you believe him?" He trusted Crystal's level-headed judgment, and wanted her opinion of Parrish's story.

"Of course I do. Matt Parrish would never kill anyone, much less the father of the girl he's about to marry!"

Stillman didn't say anything as he turned to the boiling coffeepot. He stood, retrieved the water pitcher from the cabinet, and poured water into the pot, to settle the grounds. When he'd returned the pitcher to the cabinet, he filled two cups with coffee, handed one to Crystal, and set one on his desk.

He was remembering how testy Matt Parrish had been in town yesterday. The young rancher had obviously been more than a little anxious about the prospect of acquiring old Tom Suthern's outfit. He'd been wanting that ranch for a long time, and not only to increase his own holdings, but as a buffer between his own original spread and that of the ambitious, imperialistic Blacklaws family. Parrish hadn't said as much to Stillman, but the sheriff inferred it from Parrish's feud with the Blacklaws.

Could Matt, incensed by old Suthern's refusal to sell Anchor to him, have murdered the old man?

Crystal was reading Stillman's mind. "You think it's possible, don't you, Ben?"

Before he could answer, the office door opened. Stillman and Crystal both watched Leon McMannigle step in and close the door behind him. "A mite chilly out there," the deputy groused, his shoulders hunched from the cold. "The girls keep Mrs. Lee's place so warm it throws my thermostat off."

Seeing Crystal, Leon stopped and frowned at her, politely removing his hat. "Well, Crystal Harmon. What in the heck you doin' out so early?"

"Someone killed old Tom Suthern last night, Leon," Crystal reported somberly, holding her coffee in her lap. "Matt Parrish rode over to our place and told us all about it."

The frown lines in the deputy's mahogany forehead deepened. "Huh? What? Matt Parrish?"

When Crystal had repeated the story for McMannigle, Stillman could tell Leon shared his own doubts and suspicions. So could Crystal. "Oh, not you too, Leon?"

"What do you mean—me too?" the deputy said.

She whipped her head around, taking in both men. "You men actually believe Matt Parrish killed Tom Suthern because old Tom wouldn't sell his ranch to him?"

Stillman and McMannigle studied each other. Stillman knew Leon was thinking the same thing he was: Matt Parrish had a very short fuse. As much as Stillman didn't want to believe it—he'd always liked young Parrish, despite the man's predilection for fighting—he had to consider the possibility.

"Well, all I believe right now," he said, and tipped back the last of his coffee, "is I better get out to your ranch and talk to Parrish myself, then head over to Anchor."

"You want me to come, Ben?" Leon asked.

Stillman shook his head. "Nah, you better stay here. Keep an eye on things. I'll have the doc ride out there with me. He'll have to dig the bullets out of Suthern's hide and write up a report."

Stillman paused, thoughtful.

"What is it?" McMannigle asked.

"I was just wondering why no one from Anchor came to town to report the murder."

"Maybe all the men were too busy chasin' Parrish." Stillman removed his Henry rifle from the gun rack on the wall. "But you'd think Miss Nancy could've found someone to send. Anyway, I better get going. Crystal, you better warm up a while longer, maybe get yourself something to eat. I'd send you over to our place, but Fay's probably left for school by now."

Crystal shook her head and stood. "No, I'll ride back with you and the doc," she said, returning her cup to the cabinet. "I don't trust Jody alone with little William Ben for more than a couple hours. I don't want the little tyke picking up any habits I can't break."

Stillman and McMannigle smiled. "I'll be back before nightfall," the sheriff told his deputy as he opened the door for Crystal. "I hope."

In the Harmon barn, Matt Parrish lifted his saddle from the stall partition and hefted it onto his mare. He reached under the mare's belly for the latigo, and cinched it while ramming his knee into the mare's side, so she couldn't fill her lungs with air.

"Matt!" he heard Jody yell from across the yard.

"Damnit," Parrish groused to himself as he reached for his saddlebags. He'd hoped to have gotten out of here before Jody had finished his morning chores around the ranch yard.

Jody called again, his voice louder this time, and Parrish knew he was heading toward the barn. As Parrish tied his rifle boot to his saddle, the barn's big, double doors opened, letting in the blue-gray morning light.

"Matt, what're you doin'?" Jody said, standing in the open doorway, peering into the shadows where Parrish worked on his horse.

His face flushed with consternation over this entire affair—he hadn't slept a wink last night, but stayed up pacing the living room floor—Parrish rammed his rifle into the saddle boot and turned around toward Jody.

"I've decided to ride on out of here," he said with grim defiance. "I know I said I'd stay and wait for Stillman, but I just can't. I have to ride back to Anchor—I never should've left in the first place. I have to talk to Nancy, make sure she knows I didn't kill her old man."

"That's ridiculous, Matt," Jody said. "Her riders won't let you get within two miles of that place."

"I aim to cut cross-country, ride up to the house from the backside. Most of the men are probably still out scouring the country for me anyway."

"They'll find you and hang you, Matt."

"It's a chance I have to take, Jody," Parrish said, gazing at young Harmon gravely. "Stillman's gonna haul me off to jail. And with all the evidence against me, I won't have a chance. I'll be strung up by next Tuesday." He shook his head passionately and grabbed his horse's bridle reins. "I can't give up without a fight—without at least takin' a shot at finding the real killer."

Jody shook his head. "Let Stillman do that. It's his job."

"Sorry, old pal," Parrish said as he backed the mare out of its stall. He gave a dry chuckle. "Hell, if I didn't know better, *I'd* say I was guilty!"

As Parrish began leading the mare toward the doors, Jody stepped in front of him, holding his open hand out against Parrish's chest. "I can't let you do this, Matt. Not only does it look like you're running, it's suicide."

"Get out of the way, Jody," Parrish said.

Jody shook his head. "You're stayin' here, Matt. You're out of your head."

Parrish stared at Jody, then took a deep breath, turning to his horse thoughtfully. Before Jody realized what was coming, Parrish had whipped around, planting a right cross on Jody's chin. Young Harmon was thrown to his right, falling over an oat bin and several feed sacks, red lights dancing in his eyes.

"Sorry, Jody. I'll make it up to you later," he heard Parrish say.

Shaking the cobwebs out of his head, Jody looked up to see Parrish quickly leading the mare out of the barn, then jumping onto his saddle. In a moment, he and the mare were galloping across the yard and through the main gate, heading east toward the divide and Three-Witch Valley.

7

IT WAS ABOUT ten-fifteen by Stillman's pocket watch when he, Crystal, and Doc Evans dropped into the valley of White-Tail Creek and passed through the Harmon ranch gate.

"I just hope young Harmon has some coffee on the range," Evans grumbled.

Stillman had awakened the man from a deep sleep. Evans had stayed up gambling and drinking half the night with McMannigle and several other regulars at Mrs. Lee's place. When he'd gone home, he hadn't gone alone, and Stillman had awakened the buxom brunette in the doctor's bed as well. The sheriff had discovered that the brunette wasn't nearly as friendly at eight-thirty in the morning as she was at eight-thirty at night.

"You mean you're not over that bottle flu yet, Doc?" Crystal asked.

"This ride's made it worse," Evans said. His shabby bowler was tipped low, to shield his eyes from the sun that shone brightly after the clouds had cleared. "And the sheriff here didn't allow me time for even one cup of coffee before razzing me out of my house."

Stillman reined his big bay up to the hitch rack before the Harmon cabin. "Sorry, Doc, but I'm gonna need you to look over Suthern's bullet wounds and pull the slugs from the body. No sense having him hauled all the way to town when I'm sure Miss Nancy wants him buried right there."

Evans only grumbled at this. As Stillman dismounted, the cabin door opened and Jody appeared, a crestfallen expression on his olive-skinned face.

"Hello, Ben. Doc," he greeted the men grimly. "We've brought you out here on a wild-goose chase, I'm afraid. Matt's done flown the coop."

"What?" Crystal exclaimed.

Jody nodded. "Rode out of here about twenty minutes ago. Headin' for Anchor. Gave me a nice jawbreaker before he left," he added, rubbing his chin.

"Why's he going back to Anchor?" Stillman said. "He think they feel any better about him today than they did last night?"

Jody shook his head. "The damn fool's all mixed up about it. Now he's thinkin' he should have stayed and explained himself, though how he could've done that with Otero shootin' at him, I don't know. But he thinks he can sneak back and see Nancy, convince her he didn't kill her pa, and maybe get a clue from her as to who might've pulled the trigger."

"That idiot!" Crystal exclaimed, taking the words right out of Stillman's mouth. "He's gonna get himself killed."

Stillman sighed. "Hold on, Doc," he told the doctor, who was tying his reins to the hitch rack. "We have to get over to Anchor pronto."

The doctor looked at Stillman with indignation. "The hell you say! I need a cup of coffee before I ride one more step."

"No time for that, Doc," Stillman said, climbing back aboard Sweets. "Mount up. We're outta here."

"Be careful, Ben," Crystal said as she stepped onto the porch with Jody.

"Just one cup, Ben, please," the doctor beseeched Stillman with an air of desperation.

Stillman was already riding for the gate. "Come on, Doc," he called over his shoulder. "See ye later, young'uns. Jody, I hope that chin don't grieve you too bad. Say hi to my godson for me, will you?"

Evans cursed and climbed heavily into his saddle. "I do believe he likes seeing me miserable," he grumbled, reining his skewbald away from the hitch rack. "Just wait till he needs doctoring again. Then he's gonna wish he'd let me have that coffee!"

"You're a goddamn slave driver, Stillman," Evans fairly yelled at the sheriff. "You know that?"

"What's the problem now, Doc?" Stillman said, turning to look at the doctor behind him.

They'd crossed the divide and were now making their way along a wagon trail, heading east and splitting Three-Witch Valley right down the middle. A creek bubbled to their right, and the day had warmed up enough so that Stillman had tied his coat behind his saddle and rolled his sleeves up his tanned muscle-corded forearms.

"You said we'd stop once we crossed the divide."

Stillman nodded. "That I did, Doc. Sorry. I'd just like to catch up to Matt before one of the Anchor riders does."

"I can understand that," Evans testily allowed, "but I don't normally ride a saddle. My headache finally went away, but it's been replaced by a damn sore ass. Now, I'm gonna take a break, and if you don't like it, you can plumb go to hell!"

Grinning, Stillman said, "Okay, okay, Doc. I get your drift. We'll water the horses at the creek over here, and take ten minutes to rest your ailing caboose."

"It's about time," Evans said, reining his horse off the trail and following Stillman to the brush-and-willow-choked creek. "Get a man out of bed at eight o'clock in the morning, don't allow him even one cup of coffee, and have him trailing all over the blasted county . . ."

They watered their horses, then tied them to a lightning-marred box elder. Stillman built a smoke while Evans turned to relieve himself. The sheriff's fingers halted their work at the brown paper when he thought he heard something in the distance.

He listened.

"Did you hear that, Doc?"

"Hear what?" Evans said, his back to him, one hand on his hip as he evacuated his bladder. "It was probably me, farting."

"Shhh." Stillman was still listening. Finally, he dropped the half-made quirley and started walking downstream. "You stay here with the horses. I'm gonna have a look around."

"You do that," Evans said. "Take your time."

Stillman walked along the stream, his eyes sweeping both sides of the valley. He could have sworn he'd heard a man's voice on the breeze.

A rifle cracked nearby, and the slug spanged off a rock in the creek, over Stillman's right shoulder. Stillman ducked and bolted into the willows, bulling through the weeds with his forearms held high, shielding his face.

The rifle cracked again, and the slug tore through the weeds three feet behind him.

Stillman turned toward the creek and bulled his way through the weeds to the water. Splashing into the water, he crouched behind a large glacial boulder nestled in the cattails, its base slick with moss. He drew his Colt and cursed as he pondered how to play this.

He'd been bushwhacked before, and nothing made him fouler. Whoever it was—and he suspected it was one or more Anchor riders gunning for Matt Parrish—was going to pay for his sins with a perforated hide at the most, a night in jail at the very least.

Staying low, he pushed off the rock and waded along the slow-moving creek, sliding regular looks behind and before him. When he'd walked about a hundred yards, he found a game trail through the weeds, and followed it, crouching, keeping his head below the gently bending, rasping cattails. He had to move slowly, for his wet boots squawked with every step.

When he came to the edge of the weeds, he dropped to a knee and looked around. Swinging his gaze right, he saw two men hunkered behind a knoll about fifty yards away, peering over the weeds along the creek. Both men were dressed in trail garb, and they were holding Winchesters. Two horses tied to chokecherry shrubs nibbled grass at the bottom of the knoll.

Stillman ran straight out from the weeds, then arced around behind the two men, slowing to a careful walk through the short, sun-cured grass spotted with dried cow pies. He heard the men speak to each other as they studied the creek, looking for him.

When he came to within thirty feet, he stopped, his Colt extended, the hammer back. "I'm right behind you, you stupid sons o' bitches. Don't even think about turning around before you've dropped those rifles."

The surprised horses whinnied and stomped. One of the men froze, but the other swung his Winchester around. Stillman triggered the Colt. As his slug punched through the gunman's arm, the man squeezed the rifle's trigger and dropped it, the slug tearing into the ground a few feet from his boots.

The other man whipped his head toward Stillman, fear and exasperation in his eyes.

"You want some of this?" Stillman asked him.

The man stared hard at Stillman. Then his eyes found Stillman's badge, and he shook his head. "We figured you was Parrish," he grumbled.

"You shot me, you son of a bitch!" the other man wailed, rolling around on his butt and clutching his upper arm from which blood oozed.

"I'm gonna do the same to your friend there if he doesn't drop that Winchester."

The second man dropped the Winchester and squared his shoulders at Stillman. "I told you, Sheriff. We thought you were Parrish."

"I don't care who you thought I was," Stillman said

tightly. "Getting gulched rubs my fur in the wrong direction. You boys from Anchor?"

"That's right," the second cowboy replied above his partner's grunts and curses. "Parrish killed ole Tom Suthern. We been lookin' for him since last night."

"I don't suppose you ever thought of reporting it to the law," Stillman said dryly.

"Didn't see no need," the wounded man said, lifting his head to the sheriff, his eyes slitted and his cheeks flushed with pain. "We know he did it. Otero seen him by the body with a gun in his hands. Why bother with the law?"

Stillman just scowled at the two men reproachfully. He saw that the rumors about Suthern having had to hire any man he could find, however disreputable, were true. There was no reasoning with such vipers as these. The way they saw it, the remotest chance that Parrish was guilty of Suthern's murder was reason enough to backshoot him or hang him, forgetting that a man was innocent until proven guilty. But then, they probably knew as much about the law as Stillman knew about the dark side of the moon.

"Where are the other Anchor riders?" Stillman asked them, disdain still plain in his voice.

The second man glanced around and shrugged. "I don't know. We split into pairs last night. We're gonna meet back at the ranch around noon."

Stillman nodded. "Toss those pistols into the grass and get to your feet—both of you."

"Where we goin'?" the wounded man asked.

"You don't want to be late for your rendezvous, do you?"

The wounded man cursed and aimed a fiery gaze at Stillman. "My arm needs tending, or I'm liable to bleed to death!"

Before the sheriff could answer the man, he heard, "Ben, you all right?"

He peered around the knoll. Doc Evans was walking this way, his double-barreled goose gun in his arms.

Stillman turned to the wounded man with a wry smile. "I reckon it's your lucky day, amigo."

• • •

Matt Parrish squatted on the pine-studded ridge overlooking the Anchor Ranch and raised his field glasses to his eyes. Adjusting the focus, he brought the buildings into view.

The ranch yard appeared deserted, no men in any of the corrals, and the doors of the blacksmith shop and stables were closed. At this time of the day, one of the men should have been firing up the cookshack range. Parrish had heard that Anchor's cook had left during one of Suthern's recent tirades over the cook's not sticking to his budget, but the men still had to eat. The absence of smoke from the cookshack chimney, as well as the scarcity of saddle stock in the main corral, meant that most or all of the men were still out looking for Parrish.

Dropping his gaze to the house, the rear of which he faced, he saw that it too looked quiet. Nancy must have been inside, though, because smoke ribboned from the kitchen's brick chimney.

Taking another careful look around, Parrish decided the yard was relatively safe. The Anchor men wouldn't be expecting him to circle back, to revisit the scene of the crime from which he'd fled only a few hours ago.

He turned, walked to his horse, which he'd tied to a pine on the other side of the mountain, just below the crest, and dropped his field glasses into his saddlebags. Then he climbed into the saddle and gigged the horse over the mountain and down the other side, tracing a slow, zigzagging route while keeping a cautious eye on the yard below washed by the high, late-morning sun.

As he made the base of the ridge, Parrish dismounted and tethered the mare in the pine lot at the edge of the backyard, behind one of three woodsheds. He then made his way to the house's back door, keeping his gun in its holster.

Cupping his hands around the glass, he peered into one of the door's four windowpanes. The kitchen appeared vacant, although a kettle of soup or stew steamed on the range to Parrish's right. On a tray on one of the counters, bun dough appeared ready for the oven.

Gently, Parrish turned the doorknob. The door opened, and Parrish stepped inside.

"Don't you come one step closer, Matt Parrish," a female voice said on his left. Turning that way, he saw Nancy standing in a corner with a shotgun in her arms, leveled at Parrish's chest. "If you do, I'll blow you to Kingdom Come!"

8

"NANCY, PLEASE!" PARRISH said, raising his hands placatingly. "I didn't do it."

"How could you?" the girl cried, tears streaming down her cheeks. "You killed him. You killed my father!"

"Nancy, no. I didn't," Parrish beseeched her shaking his head, his heart breaking for her. Not only had her father been murdered, but her future husband had been deemed the killer. "I heard the shots and rode over to the creek. I found him there, on his walking path by the water."

"Otero said you had your gun drawn," Nancy said with defiance mixed with sadness.

Parrish nodded. "Sure I'd drawn my gun. Someone had killed your father. I figured the man was still in the woods somewhere. I thought maybe he'd take a shot at me, so . . ." He spread his hands helplessly. "Nancy, what was I supposed to do?"

"So you *ran*? Why did you run?"

"I ran because Otero was shooting at me and because I knew how it must have looked, me with my gun out and your father lying there dead. I realize now that I should have stayed and taken my chances. Your father's men probably would have hung me from the nearest tree, but at least I wouldn't have looked as guilty as I do now."

The accusatory look in Nancy's eyes flagged. The shotgun wilted in her arms, and she lowered it. Parrish started toward her, but she half-raised the gun again and said, "No, Matt, stay away," and that stopped him.

Moving stiffly past him, she took a seat at the food-preparation table, laying the shotgun across her lap, unwilling to let go of it, it appeared, in case she still needed it. She set her elbows on the table, brought her face to her hands, and sobbed.

"My father is dead! Oh, God!"

Parrish looked at her, wanting to move to her and comfort her, but knowing he could not. Not until she believed his story. In the meantime, he had to settle for: "I'm so sorry, Nancy. I'll admit I was frustrated when I left here last night, but I certainly wasn't frustrated enough to kill your father. Why would I kill him? I love *you!*"

Nancy dropped her hands from her face, and crossed her arms on the table. Staring through tears at the smeared flour and sugar on the oilcloth, she said, "At first, after Otero came and told me, I didn't believe it was true. But then, after the men had gone off—I hadn't been able to stop them—I remembered what a temper you have."

She turned to him. "Remember when we were at that dance at the Logan Creek Ranch, Matt? Remember when Sy Kirby got a little tight and asked me to dance a few times?"

"More like five or six, after you'd danced with him twice already," Parrish grumbled.

"For whatever reason, Matt, do you remember how belligerent you got, and how you and Sy nearly came to blows right there in the barn until several of the men hustled you both outside?"

Parrish gazed at her with deep frustration and remorse. "Nancy, I was drinking that night. I know that's no excuse, and I really try to control my temper. . . ." His voice trailed off, and he sighed. He knew how inadequate and desperate his words sounded. He pulled a chair out from the table, and sat across from her, leaning back in the chair, his shoulders slumped. "All I can tell you, Nancy, is yes, I have a temper. But I did not kill your father. I promise you that."

She stared at him dully for a long time. Then her eyebrows beetled. "Who then?"

"I think one of the Anchor riders did it. Maybe even Otero himself."

Nancy's eyes widened with shock. "Why?"

Parrish raised his hands and dropped them to his knees. "You know how your father was getting. He was hard to work for. Talk about temper tantrums! Heck, several from his old crew even came to me looking for work. . . ."

Nancy turned her head to the side and dropped her eyes, apparently considering the possibility that one of her father's own men had killed him. The kettle on the stove bubbled, and she looked at it, as if suddenly just remembering it was there.

"I made some stew," she said, in a small, faraway voice. "I had to do something . . . to keep busy."

Parrish didn't say anything. After a while, she turned her stricken gaze back to him. "Matt Parish," she said quietly, "you look me straight in the eye and you tell me for certain you did not kill my father."

"Nancy, I swear on my own parents' graves and on the date we've planned for our wedding, I did not kill your father." He stared at her with a flinty sincerity. "You have to believe me, Nancy. I love you and I want us to spend the rest of our lives together."

Nancy sighed. Her voice quaked as she said, "Oh, Matt, I want to believe you. Really I do. More than anything in the world."

"Then do."

Emotion overcame her once again, and she raised her hands to her face, bawling. Parrish got up from his chair and walked around the table. He squatted down on his haunches and took one of her hands in his.

"Nancy," he said, "I'm sorry to bring this up right now, because I know how sad and lost you must feel. But I'm pretty sure Ben Stillman is on his way here, to take me in.

Before he gets here, I have to know something. I have to know if you have any reason at all to believe that any one of your father's men in particular might have wanted him dead."

Choking back sobs and wiping the tears from her swollen cheeks with her free hand, Nancy shook her head and said, "No."

"I'm sorry, Nancy, but I have to ask you one more hard question. Do you think Tommy could have done it?"

"Why, you goddamn murderin' bastard."

Parrish turned to see Tommy walk into the kitchen, one of his pearl-handled Colts extended in his right hand, its hammer thumbed back. The barrel was aimed at Parrish's head.

"Tommy!" Nancy cried.

"Just you keep quiet, sister. This son of a bitch murdered our father, no matter how hard he's tried to convince you otherwise." The young man's eyes burned a hole through Parrish. His hair was rumpled and his face was creased and pale, as though he'd just awakened from a drunken stupor. He wore black jeans, boots, and his black cartridge belt and double holsters. A long underwear top, washed out and threadbare, served as his shirt.

Parrish figured the young firebrand had returned home late last night to hear the news his father had been killed. Too drunk to ride after Parrish with the others, he'd no doubt passed out in his bed. He must have awakened to Parrish and Nancy talking in the kitchen.

"Take it easy, Tommy," Parrish said, slowly straightening his legs and holding his hands out from his sides. "Just take it easy."

"No, you take it easy, you son of a bitch. What kind of fool talk you been filling her head with anyway?" He jerked his chin at his sister.

"I've been telling Nancy the truth," Parrish insisted. "I did not kill your father. It may look like I did, but I didn't."

Tommy smirked knowingly, slowly nodding his head. "No, you killed him, all right. 'Cause he wouldn't sell to you. So you killed him before I had time to convince him to write me back into his will, so Anchor would go to Nancy and then, after you were married, to you."

"Oh, God!" Nancy cried, overcome once again, not knowing what to believe. She dropped her head in her arms on the table and wailed.

"It's not true, Nancy," Parrish assured her. "None of it's true." He looked at Tommy, hate flashing in the kid's eyes. "What about you, Tommy? You had more reason to kill your father than I did. Anchor would have gone to Nancy anyway after his death. You were written out of the will. Maybe you killed him out of spite."

"Don't listen to him, Nancy!" the young whip fairly raged, spittle flying from his lips. "He's just tryin' to confuse you, make it look like I done it when he knows he's the one . . . he's the one who killed Pa." He jerked the gun at Parrish and took two steps to his right. "Get outside. We're goin' out the front."

Nancy lifted her head from the table, turning her anguished gaze to her brother. "What are you going to do?"

"I'm takin' your boyfriend outside, deal him a little frontier justice."

Before Nancy could respond, Parrish said spitefully, not sure what the kid had in mind but knowing he wouldn't like it, "You've been reading too many stories, Tommy."

"Get out there. Now! Or I'll shoot you right here."

"Tommy, no!" Nancy wailed. "You can't!"

Tommy jerked his fiery eyes at her. "Shut up, I told you! I'm in charge around here now." To Parrish, he shouted so loudly his voice cracked, "I told you to git!"

Parrish thought it over. He could tell from the kid's eyes that he meant business. Figuring he might be able to get the jump on him later, before Tommy did whatever he had in his wicked little brain, Parrish started forward. As he passed Tommy, the kid grabbed the gun from Parrish's holster and stepped quickly back, out of range of Parrish's fists.

The kid was canny—you had to give him that, Parrish thought as he moved through the kitchen door. He walked stiffly down the hall and through the parlor, feeling the occasional poke of Tommy's gun in his back. But when Parrish glanced at the kid over his shoulder, Tommy was too far behind him to make feasible a quick swing with his arms or a kick with his legs. Not without getting shot anyway.

Parrish moved through the foyer, and in a few seconds he was on the porch, staring out across the ranch yard with its scattered log buildings and corrals, bleached gray and looking tumbledown under the noonday sun, their worn and missing shingles more obvious in this light. In the distant pasture, two mutts were hunting gophers, digging with their butts in the air, tails wagging. Parrish stared at them, wondering with a vague irony if they would be the last images of this world he'd take to his grave.

Wondering if it was his fate to be remembered by the living as the man who'd murdered old Tom Suthern ...

"Keep movin', Parrish," Tommy ordered, poking his gun in the rancher's back once again, shoving him toward the steps.

Parrish took one step and then stopped, having heard the hoofbeats to his right. Turning that way, he saw several riders emerge from the lane connecting the headquarters to the main road. There were six of them, Parrish saw. The Anchor riders, dusty and tired, slouching in their saddles as they returned from their nightlong search. Well, now I'm finished for sure, Parrish thought, dread like hot oil washing over him.

The black-clad Otero was in the lead. Seeing Parrish and young Suthern on the porch, he reined his gelding that way. The other riders, swinging their heads toward the house, followed suit. Indignant curses and mutters rose above the clomp of the horses' hooves and the squeak of the tack. The men's expressions rode the gamut between surprise and exasperation.

"Where the hell did you find him, Tommy?" Otero asked as he reined up before the porch, the other riders clustering behind him.

Parrish saw the Anchor foreman, Charlie Klosterman, sitting a buckskin to Otero's right and slightly behind. He had the cowed demeanor of an old wolf whose power had been usurped by one of the lesser, rowdier males in the pack. Klosterman had been Suthern's foreman for ten years. He was the most senior rider here, and supposedly the man in charge.

But that wasn't how it was, Parrish saw. The third in command, Otero, was obviously the one calling the shots.

"I found him in my own kitchen," Tommy said snidely. "He slipped in right under your nose, Otero. What were you boys doing out there anyway, taking a pleasure ride?"

Otero flushed. "I was scouting south. He musta come in from the north." He swiveled a look behind him, and two riders flanking the pack acquired sheepish expressions on their unshaven faces.

Turning back to Tommy, Otero said, "Well, let's string the bastard up, eh?" He looked at Parrish and grinned eagerly. "Deserves it, no? Thinkin' he can get by with dry-gulching a poor old man." He followed up the statement by shaking his head ostentatiously.

" 'Poor old man,' " said one of the other men, quietly chuckling.

"Hey, shut your damn mouth!" Tommy yelled, his features flushing with self-righteous indignation. "Whatever my old man may have been, he's dead, and you'll show him some respect. If you're plannin' on stayin' on here, that is."

Parrish half-turned to the young man behind him. "You callin' the shots now, Tommy? I thought you were written out of the will."

Detecting the mockery in Parrish's tone, the kid took a step forward and slammed his revolver against the back of Parrish's head. Lights flashing in his eyes, Parrish dropped to his knees with a pained grunt, clamping a hand to his torn scalp.

Tommy bent over him. "Only because you didn't give him a chance to change it!" Tommy yelled. "He would have. He was about to—I know he was. Anyways, it don't matter. Nancy can't run this spread alone, and she sure as hell ain't gonna turn it over to you, you murderin' son of a bitch!" With that, the young man kicked Parrish in the ribs. The blow sent the rancher tumbling down the porch steps and landing in the yard with another groan, clutching his side.

"Tommy!" Nancy yelled from the doorway. "Stop it!"

"Go back inside, sister," Tommy ordered. "I'm the one in charge now."

Despite Nancy's protests, Tommy shoved her back inside the house, returned to the porch, and slammed the door behind him. Regarding Otero, he said, "Take him over to the cottonwoods by the creek and string the bastard up!"

Otero chuckled as he removed the lariat from his saddle and began shaking out a loop.

Klosterman finally spoke up. "Tommy, you can't hang the man. Turn him over to the law, for godsakes. Let Stillman handle it."

"We don't need Stillman," Tommy said, aiming his hatchet face at the middle-aged foreman. "He killed my pa on Anchor land, and he'll swing on Anchor land. Besides, everyone knows he's buddies with Stillman and McMannigle. Hell, they'll probably just turn him loose."

Biting his lower lip, his pale eyes dark with consternation, Klosterman shook his head. "It ain't right, Tommy. Matt should go before a judge and a jury. It just ain't right. What's more, it's against the law."

"If you ain't got the stomach for frontier justice, Charlie," Tommy said, glowering, "then you can ride on out of here. I only want men with spine on my roll."

The foreman stared at the diabolical youth, the lines in his face dissolving along with his resolve. Klosterman was middle-aged in a young man's profession. Besides that, his hips were bad. If he left Anchor, he was as good as finished.

He shook his head and dropped his eyes, feeling feeble. "Do what you have to," he murmured, hating himself. "But I won't have no part in it." He spat a string of chew and, his paunch drawing his shoulders down, reined his chestnut gelding toward the stables.

Pain shooting through his ribs as well as his skull, Parrish watched the old foreman go, knowing Klosterman had been his last hope, however slight. Otero laughed and settled a loop over Parrish's head, drawing it tight around his shoulders.

"Come on, amigos, we have justice to serve!" he yelled to the others, turning his horse around and giving Parrish a savage lurch.

To avoid being dragged as Otero rode toward the creek, Parrish heaved himself to his feet and stumbled along behind the Mexican's cantering horse, the rope drawn tight around his arms. He wished now he'd stayed away from here, that he'd let Stillman do the dirty work.

But wishing wasn't going to get him anywhere. He had to do something before these hardcases played cat's cradle with his head.

But what could he do? There were a half-dozen other Anchor men accompanying him and Otero to the creek. Even if Parrish's hands were free, he had no gun or even a knife.

The hopelessness of his situation had turned his knees to mud, and his heart thudded painfully in his chest, sweat breaking out on his face and down his back. At the same time, he felt a January cold invade his limbs, all the way to his fingers and toes. It was a bone-deep chill spawned by desperation and fear.

Otero halted his horse by a big cottonwood at the edge of the ranch yard and dismounted. Tossing his reins to one of the other riders, he walked toward Parrish, a smirk twisting his thin, cracked lips and twitching his mustache. "Now, you're gonna get on my horse, *comprende*? After I tie a noose around your neck."

As the Mexican approached, Parrish swung his right foot behind him, then brought it forward and up with a sudden spurt of angry energy. The toe of his boot connected soundly with the Mexican's groin.

"Ahhh!" Otero cried, bringing his gloved hands to his crotch as he bent forward at the waist. *"Madre de dios!"*

Before Parrish could lash out at the man again, one of the other riders gigged his horse to him quickly, and butted his head with a Winchester. Parrish fell and rolled. Looking up, he saw Otero straighten, his face turning even more savage than before, with no trace of his previous humor. The Mexican unsnapped the safety thong over his low-slung revolver, and began drawing the gun from his holster.

Before the gun cleared leather, a rifle cracked. Otero's mouth opened with a startled grunt and his right knee bent as he dropped his revolver and grabbed his calf.

"What the h—" the man who'd slugged Parrish said with a bewildered air, hunching his shoulders defensively and looking around.

"Pick up the gun, Otero," a man said in a slow, almost disinterested voice. "And I'll blow you so full of holes you won't hold a thimbleful of tequila."

Parrish looked where all the other men were gazing. Ben Stillman approached on his big bay, the butt of a Henry rifle snugged against his thigh.

9

SEEING THE SHERIFF, Otero dropped to his butt, clutching his bloody calf with both hands and cursing in Spanish.

"The rest of you men throw all your weapons in a pile right there." Stillman approached the group, indicating the ground with the barrel of his Henry. He knew he was liable to get himself shot, riding solo into this hanging committee, outnumbered six to one, but he saw no other way. The Anchor riders were about to leave Parrish doing a midair ballet.

The Anchor men sneered at Stillman.

Stillman raised the Henry and shot a hat off a head. The best way to cow a group like this was to act even more enraged than they were.

"Shit!" the man groused, watching his hat tumble to the grass behind him. To the others, he said, "Throw your guns down. He's pure loco."

"Parrish killed Mr. Suthern!" Otero yelled at Stillman.

"Did you see him do it?" Stillman asked as the men reluctantly tossed their weapons on the ground.

"You bet I seen him. Shot the old man twice—once in

the neck, once in the head. Blood all over the place."

"He's lying, Ben!" Parrish objected. He'd lifted the rope over his head and stood with his arms free, facing Stillman. "He didn't see no such thing, because I didn't do it! I heard the shots, and I rode over to the creek. Otero himself probably shot him."

"He murdered my pa, Stillman," Tommy Suthern yelled as he walked out from the house, tucking the tail of a bib-front shirt into his pants. "I gave the order to hang him."

Stillman grunted. "You did, did you?"

"That's right. Why waste time with a judge and jury? Otero saw the whole thing. Parrish shot my old man in a rage because Pa wouldn't sell to him."

Parrish opened his mouth to speak, but Stillman cut him off. "Okay, okay," he said. "I'll sort through it later. In the meantime, I want you Anchor men to hightail it over to the bunkhouse. Two of you help your friend Otero here. If I see so much as a nose poke out the door before I'm out of here with Parrish, I'm gonna shoot it off."

Turning to young Suthern, Stillman said, "Tommy, toss your gun down. I want you in the bunkhouse with the others."

The kid just stared at Stillman, his eyes dark, a rage building deep within them.

Stillman returned the gaze, the breeze fluttering his green neckerchief. "Tommy, I'm sorry about what happened to your pa, but I'm not going to pretend I like you, because I don't. You best toss that gun down and head for the bunkhouse, or I'm gonna climb out of this saddle and slap the holy shit out of you."

Young Suthern's eyes bunched and his nostrils flared. He balled his fists at his sides, then released them. With a caustic snort, he finally tossed his gun down with the others and said, "This ain't finished, Stillman. Not by a long shot." Then he turned and headed for the bunkhouse.

Stillman heard a horse blow, and swiveled to look behind him. Doc Evans and the two bushwhackers were heading his way. Stillman had told Evans to wait with the two men down by the main gate, with orders to shoot if they got frisky. The bushwhackers rode abreast, the wounded one's bandaged right arm in a sling. Evans brought up the rear, his bird gun in the crook of his arm.

"You two follow the others to the bunkhouse," Stillman told the bushwhackers.

"You ain't gonna take us in?" the wounded man asked hopefully.

"Get moving before I change my mind," Stillman warned, raising his rifle. He had such a big mess to sift through here that he didn't want to waste any time on the bushwhackers.

"All right, all right," the other man said. He and the wounded rider spurred their horses toward the stables.

Evans rode up to Stillman and stared after Otero, being helped to the bunkhouse by two of the other riders.

"Now I suppose you want me to tend the Mex?"

"If you would, Doc."

"Damnit, Ben," the doctor complained. "Will you stop giving me so damn much work to do? I haven't had a single cup of coffee yet today." Grumbling, Evans followed the Anchor men to the bunkhouse.

Parrish looked at Stillman. "What about me, Ben?"

Stillman drew a ragged breath. "I'm afraid I'm going to have to arrest you, Matt," he said, reaching into his saddlebags for handcuffs. Tossing the cuffs to Matt, he said, "Put those on."

"Ben, I told you—"

"I know what you told me," Stillman said. "Put the cuffs on, and don't try to get away from me. Running just makes you look all the more guilty, and you already look guilty as hell."

Parrish sighed and clamped the cuffs to his wrists.

"Now head for the house," Stillman told him. "I want to speak to Nancy and check Suthern out for myself."

As Parrish started away, Stillman heeled Sweets after him. What a goddamn mess. The sheriff shifted his head to roll the kinks out of his neck. He was getting a headache, and he had a feeling it was only going to get worse.

•   •   •

Nancy Suthern dabbed at her eyes with a lacy pink handkerchief and said, "I was in the kitchen, filling a plate for Dad to eat later, when I heard the shots. I thought it was just one of the men shooting a coyote or one of the wolves that have been prowling the ravine east of the house. But then I heard yelling, so I went to a window and saw several of the men running toward the creek. That's when I got worried."

She gently blew her nose. Matt Parrish, sitting beside her on the parlor sofa, patted her shoulder awkwardly with his manacled hands. Stillman sat in the straight-back, damask-upholstered chair he'd pulled near Nancy, his hat in his lap and a sympathetic softness to his gaze.

"Dad often walked out by the creek when he was upset about something, and after his and Matt's argument, he was pretty upset. Just a few minutes earlier, though, I thought I'd heard him upstairs, so I didn't go outside until later. That's when I saw the men running back from the creek to the stables. I stopped Charlie Klosterman and asked him what was wrong and he told me—" She stopped as her shoulders shook, and she sobbed.

"I take it you didn't see anyone suspicious in the yard or heading toward the creek then?" Stillman said.

Nancy shook her head as she stared at the moist hanky in her lap. "No. No one."

Parrish cleared his throat. "Nancy, do you have any idea who'd want to see your father killed? Anyone at all? I mean, had he had any arguments with any of the men recently?" There was an air of desperation to the rancher's questions.

Nancy shrugged and looked at him, gave a wan smile. "You know Dad, Matt. He was getting more and more surly every day. But no, I can't remember him getting into it with anyone recently. Except"—she stopped and dropped her gaze guiltily—"except for you, of course."

Parrish frowned, sheepish, and glanced at Stillman, whose face was implacable. Then Nancy spun to Parrish quickly and said, "But I know you didn't do it, Matt. I'm sorry for doubting you before. It's just that . . . Dad had just been killed and I kept remembering the argument. But I know now you wouldn't have killed my father, no matter how much you wanted the ranch."

She turned to Stillman and said it again. "I just know Matt didn't do it, Sheriff. I just know it."

Stillman didn't reply to that. As much as he wanted to, he didn't know if he believed young Parrish or not. Matt had a fiery temper. He was downright out of control at times. If old Suthern had pushed him too far, said the wrong things . . .

He certainly looked innocent, Stillman thought as he studied the young rancher. But many a guilty man had worn an innocent face.

Turning to Nancy, Stillman said, "Thanks for your help, Miss Suthern. Again, I'm terribly sorry about your father. I had a lot of respect for him."

"I hope you find who killed him."

"I will," Stillman said. "Don't you worry. I'll get to the bottom of it."

As he stood, he heard the front door open.

"Anyone here?" Doc Evans called.

To Nancy, Stillman said, "I'll take care of it," and left the parlor. He found Evans in the foyer toting his black medical kit.

"How's Otero?" Stillman asked.

Evans chuckled. "Mad as a bullet-burned Mexican."

"It's not serious?"

Evans shook his head. "Just a flesh wound. I wrapped it up. It'll sting for a while, but those boys have enough whiskey in the bunkhouse to kill the pain." Evan shook his head. "All that whiskey, and they never offered me a drop."

Stillman smiled. "I'm sure it's nothing personal."

"No, I have a feeling it's the company I keep," Evans said, regarding Stillman wryly. "Well, where's old Tom? I'll dig those bullets out of him and see what caliber gun the killer used."

Stillman looked amazed. "Without balking? I thought you were going to demand some coffee first."

"The notion plumb left me. Now I just want to get home for a drink."

Stillman shook his head and pointed down the hall opening on the doctor's left. "His study is right down there. Nancy had the men lay him out in there, on a sofa."

"I'll just be a minute or two," Evans said, starting down the hall.

"Matt and I will be out at the creek," Stillman called. "Meet us out there when you're done."

The doctor lifted an arm in acknowledgment and turned into the study. Stillman returned to the parlor, where Parrish and Nancy were still seated on the divan, speaking in hushed tones. Stillman hated to interrupt them, but he still had work to do before heading back to Clantick.

He cleared his throat before saying, "We best get a move on, Matt. I want you to show me where you found Mr. Suthern." To Nancy, he said, "Are you going to be all right out here, Miss Suthern?"

"I'll be fine, Sheriff," Nancy said.

"Are you sure, Nancy?" Parrish asked her. His eyes darkened and his jaw tightened as he said, "I have a feeling there's a killer on your father's roll."

"I'll be all right, Matt," Nancy assured him. "Tommy will be here, and while I know he's not the best of citizens, he'll watch out for his sister."

"I hope you're right," Parrish said with a sigh.

Nancy turned to Stillman, her eyes pinched with anguish. "Do you have to arrest Matt, Sheriff? I just know he didn't do it."

"I'm afraid I do," Stillman said with genuine regret. "I don't like it any more than you do, Miss Suthern, but I'm afraid, under the circumstances, Matt will have to go before the judge. I'm sure there will be a hearing tomorrow, if you want to ride in for it. Whatever you have to tell the judge in Matt's defense sure couldn't hurt."

"I'll be there," Nancy said, turning to Matt and clutching his hands in hers.

Later, when Stillman and Parrish had retrieved Matt's horse, they investigated the spot by the creek where Suthern

had been killed. Stillman scoured the area for evidence—
boot prints, horse prints, shell casings—and came up with
nothing.

He was wading back to the ranch side of the creek when
Doc Evans appeared on his skewbald, his black bag
strapped to his saddle. Parrish stood handcuffed by his
horse, looking thoughtful and grim.

"What'd you get, Doc?" Stillman asked Evans.

Evans tossed him a knotted white handkerchief. Stillman
opened the cloth and inspected two pocked and dented
slugs, holding each up to the light filtering through the
trees.

"Forty-five-sixty," he said. Turning to Parrish, he said,
"What kind of rifle you carry in your saddle boot, Matt?"

"Guess."

Stillman scowled and shook his head. But the information really didn't tell him much, for the .45-60 was a common caliber. "Let's head to town," he said, moving toward
his horse.

"Aren't you gonna talk to Otero?" Parrish asked, his
brows beetled with urgency. "And what about Tommy?"

"All in good time," Stillman said as he swung onto his
saddle. "All in good time." He knew he wouldn't get anything out of the Anchor men today, as impassioned as they
all were. Tomorrow he'd question each man separately
from the others.

When Parrish had climbed atop his mare and he and
Stillman and Doc Evans were riding west, Stillman suddenly reined his bay to a halt.

"What is it, Ben?" Evans asked.

Stillman was frowning northward, at the trees along the
creek. About a hundred yards off, a man afoot was leading
a tall sorrel on a loose rein. He was scouring the ground as
if looking for something.

"Charlie Klosterman," Parrish said. "What the hell you
suppose he's doing out there?"

Stillman was wondering the same thing. Then Klosterman and his horse disappeared around a bend in the creek.

"Let's go," Stillman said, gigging his horse along the trail.

It was getting late and he needed to get back to town with his prisoner. But Charlie Klosterman would be the first man he talked to when he returned to Anchor.

10

"WHERE THE HELL you been, old hoss?" Otero asked Charlie Klosterman as the old foreman entered the bunkhouse.

Night had fallen, and the lamps were lit. A small fire ticked in the two stoves, one at each end of the long, low-raftered lodge choked with hand-sawed bunks and tables. The men were lounging around in their blankets or playing cards at a table near the front stove. The air in the room was its usual amalgam of sweat, leather, woodsmoke, and the bacon and biscuits the men had eaten for supper.

"I've been tryin' to get some work done around here," Klosterman said as he closed the door on the chill autumn night and hung his weather-beaten hat on a wall peg.

"This late?" Otero said from his bottom bunk. He was clad in only his long underwear and black hat, the doctor's bandage showing white against his dark-skinned right calf.

"Someone needs to do it. God knows you boys do little enough during the day."

"Ah, we work hard enough," Bernie Sykes said lazily as he tossed a three of spades on the table. "What's the point anyway? The old man's been dyin' for two years and now he's dead. I 'spect we're all gonna be drawin' our last wages here in a day or two."

Klosterman shrugged out of his denim coat and rolled his shirt sleeves up his arms. "Think she'll sell?"

Sykes shrugged. "What else she gonna do with this place? Turn it over to Tommy?" The little, round-faced cowboy with lazy brown eyes gave a caustic snort.

"Well, we know it ain't gonna be goin' to Parrish," Otero said with a grin.

"You really think he did it?" another cowboy, Joe Coombs, asked the Mexican. He was one of the two who'd accidentally bushwhacked Stillman earlier, and he occasionally rode the owlhoot trail with Tommy Suthern.

"Sure," Otero said. "I told you, I seen him."

Coombs shrugged and went back to reading his dime novel on his top bunk over the cardplayers. Klosterman turned to the washstand. He poured lukewarm water from a battered tin pitcher into the basin, and splashed his face, washing away the dust and sweat.

"What I've been wonderin', Otero," Klosterman said conversationally as he washed, "is how you could have seen him. I mean, what were you doin' over by the creek when it happened?"

Otero rolled his eyes toward the foreman, his face hard. "Don't you believe me, amigo?"

"I ain't sayin' I believe you or don't believe you. I'm just wonderin' what you were doin' over by the creek when Parrish supposedly killed Mr. Suthern."

"What do you mean 'supposedly'?" Coombs said. "Who else could've killed him?"

Dave Hannabe slapped a card on the table. "Ah, why don't you boys give it a rest! Ask me, the old goat had it comin'."

Klosterman lowered the towel he was drying his face on and studied the big, shaggy-headed Hannabe curiously. Then he slid a quick, furtive gaze around the room, sizing up each of the six others in turn—Coombs, Sykes, Web Landers, Steve Lacy, Andy McKenna, and "Happy" Lyle Rhodes. None were even close to the cream of Hill

County's cowboy crop. Except for Andy McKenna, all had been fired by other outfits and had been hired by old Suthern because no one else would work for him.

Klosterman didn't care for any of these men except McKenna, a stocky, good-natured lad who had come up the trail from Nebraska and who wasn't a bad horse-gentler. The kid wouldn't have killed Suthern, but he was about the only one Klosterman could rule out—besides himself, that was. Any of the others—Coombs, Sykes, Landers, Lacy, Hannabe, Rhodes, and Otero—could've pulled the trigger for the right reason. Hell, Otero, a killer born and bred if Klosterman had ever seen one, could've pulled it for no reason at all.

Of course, Parrish might have done it, like Otero claimed. The rancher certainly had the temper and the reason. But Klosterman didn't think Parrish was dumb enough to shoot Suthern so soon after an argument that had been heard all over the ranch.

Otero still hadn't said what he was doing at the creek when Suthern was shot, and Klosterman had a feeling he wasn't going to. The foreman didn't feel up to pushing the Mexican for an answer either. He'd been *segundo* here for eight years, but his authority didn't carry with this bunch, and as much as he hated to admit it, he was plumb afraid of Otero. He didn't want the crazy Mexican slashing at his throat with a razor-edged stiletto, as had happened once before.

He shook his head as he sat at a table by himself, nibbling a left-over biscuit and sipping the scorched coffee. It was just plain awful what had become of this outfit, with men on the roster like those surrounding Klosterman now. If he wasn't so old and tired, he'd pull his last wages and leave. But then, he felt a loyalty to Miss Suthern. He didn't want to abandon her to this bunch of rapscallions her father had left on his roll.

It was almost as though Otero had been reading Klosterman's thoughts.

"Ahhh," the Mexican said. "Now the lovely *señorita* is up in the big house . . . all alone."

The other men chuckled or laughed.

Hannabe said, "Yep, she's alone, all right. Seen Tommy head to town near two hours ago."

Bernie Sykes said, "Yeah, Miss Suthern's about as pretty as a Smoky Mountain sunset."

"I've always wondered what she looks like with her clothes off," Joe Coombs said over the top of his book, his eyes growing dreamy.

"So that's why you spend so much time in the privy," said the thick-bearded, shaggy-headed Hannabe as he got up to chunk more wood in the stove.

The others laughed. Coombs flushed and went back to his book.

"Maybe I'll have to find out sometime," Hannabe said around a grin. He brought a black cheroot to his lips and puffed.

"Find out what?" Klosterman asked, his eyes wary.

Hannabe turned to him grinning. "What Miss Nancy looks like under all that starch and lace."

Klosterman stared at him, feeling an angry burn in his gut. He wanted to warn the man away from the house, but Klosterman knew they'd be empty words. He wouldn't— couldn't—back them up. At least, not here, not now. But if he ever saw Hannabe heading that way, toward Miss Suthern, the big cowboy might just end up with a rusty pig-sticker in his back.

"She would be too much woman for you, amigo," Otero told Hannabe.

"How do you know?" Hannabe inquired.

"Let's just say that men of Spanish blood have an instinct for such things and leave it at that, eh?" The Mexican caught Klosterman's glance. "Eh, Charlie?" he said, mocking.

When Klosterman did not answer but only stared angrily back at the Mexican, Otero stuck his tongue out, lewdly taunting, widening his eyes like a crazy man. Then he chuckled and went back to his cheroot.

Klosterman flushed and turned away, feeling as old and feeble as he'd ever felt. When he'd finished the biscuit and coffee, he undressed and collapsed on his bunk, wishing the Good Lord would just take him now and put him out of his misery.

But first, he thought as he drew the blankets up to his chin, he wanted to know who killed Suthern. Not only to satisfy his curiosity, but to appease the sense of justice that his old age and cynicism had not yet totally dashed.

Kolsterman fell asleep listening to the fall breeze whisper through the loose chinking between the logs of the bunkhouse walls. He woke sometime later to the sound of someone rustling furtively about the room.

Klosterman lifted his head to peer through the darkness. The pale starlight penetrating the windows limned a figure to his left and two bunks down. It would be either Dave Hannabe or Steve Lacy. The man was dressing quietly, then stepping into his boots. He moved with a more furtive air than someone getting up to use a thunder mug or the privy, and Klosterman's heart picked up its pace as his curiosity grew.

The man was dressing to go somewhere.

Where would he be heading at this hour—probably close to midnight or one in the morning?

To the house? Klosterman wondered with an angry flush.

Quietly, the man stepped into the aisle between the two rows of bunks and, walking softly on the balls of his feet, moved toward the door. As he approached Klosterman's bunk, the foreman dropped his head back on the pillow, but kept his eyes open.

When the man had passed, Klosterman turned his head to watch the vague form remove a coat from one of the several pegs by the door, and pull it on. Donning a hat, he carefully, quietly opened the door.

He stepped through and pulled the door shut behind him, until the latch gently clicked in the frame.

The wind creaked the walls and the snores resounded throughout the lodge. In his sleep, Andy McKenna was calling a horse named Pickle. . . .

Klosterman lay there thinking for several minutes. Finally, he threw his covers back and stood, wincing at the stiffness in his lower back and at the ache in his knees. He looked for an empty bunk and found it: Dave Hannabe's.

Was that sneaky bastard heading for the house?

Urgently but slowly, Klosterman gathered his clothes off the wall pegs and dressed, his skin pimpling from the chill that had seeped through the walls when the stove had burned down. When he'd shrugged into his wool-lined duck coat and hat, he went out, gently latched the door behind him, and looked around.

The wind swirled leaves about the yard, and slapped an unlatched door somewhere. The barn's loft doors and the windmill squeaked. Spying movement out of the corner of his eye, Klosterman turned to see a shadow move before the stables.

It was Hannabe, leading a horse from the shed and closing the doors before stepping into the saddle. Standing back to weld his shadow with that of the bunkhouse, Klosterman watched the big, shaggy-headed man gig the horse past the windmill and stock tank, around the blacksmith shop and training corral, and down the lane toward the main gate.

If it wasn't Miss Suthern he was after, what the hell was it?

Stepping out from the bunkhouse's shadow, Klosterman lifted his collar against the chill wind and moved to the stables as fast as his old legs would allow. Inside, he saddled a pied gelding and led it outside, closed the stable doors, and climbed into the leather, giving an involuntary groan at both his weariness and the lateness of the hour.

He wasn't sure why he was doing what he was doing, but something told him he'd know once he learned where Hannabe was heading this time of the night. He didn't see how Hannabe's sneaking off in the night could have anything to do with Suthern's murder—unless the waddie was working with rustlers, that is, and the old man had become suspicious. . . .

Klosterman tossed the possibility around in his head as he gigged the gelding across the yard, nervously fingering the butt of his Smith & Wesson and spurring the horse into a lope down the lane. When he made the main road, he looked in both directions.

Seeing nothing but stars, he got down and carefully inspected the road. An Army tracker during the Indian wars, he knew fresh tracks when he saw them, and seeing them now in the starlight reflected off the clay-colored road, he climbed back into the saddle and gigged the pie into a westward canter, staring cautiously ahead as he watched for Hannabe.

The last thing he wanted to do was ride into a rustlers' camp and get his ass shot off.

When he'd ridden a mile along the road, the vague form of a horse and rider appeared about fifty yards ahead, starlight winking off the rider's spurs and silver-studded hatband. Keeping his distance, Klosterman followed, frowning and holding his collar closed at his throat.

Soon Hannabe turned off the main road, taking an old horse trail, and Klosterman found himself traversing rough country, treacherous at night, until Vasserman's stage stop and roadhouse appeared in a hollow below him. Horses in the corral nickered suspiciously, and Klosterman saw a horse and rider, vaguely revealed by the lamplit windows, approach the cabin and stop at the hitching post.

Hannabe dismounted, looped his reins over the tie rack, mounted the narrow boardwalk that served as a stoop, and opened the door. A wedge of lamplight fell on the stoop, then disappeared when Hannabe stepped inside and closed the door.

Klosterman studied the roadhouse for several minutes. Hoyt Vasserman, the man who ran the place, had a whore or two working for him now and then, but Klosterman doubted Hannabe would have ridden all this way at this hour to visit a whore.

No, there had to be more to it than that, Klosterman thought as he gigged his horse down the hill. When he came to within thirty yards of the cabin, he dismounted and tied the pie to some brush, then stole along the trail, ignoring the creaks in his aching bones, and flattened his back against the rear wall of the roadhouse.

Snugging his ear to the wood, he listened.

There was a voice, but he couldn't make out any words. Deciding to head around to the front, he edged around the cabin's corner, made his way along the side, and turned left, crouching under a window and whispering acquiescently to the two horses tethered to the hitch rack. They bobbed their heads and twitched their ears, dubious.

Removing his hat, Klosterman peered through the window. The room, outfitted with several long tables and benches, was nearly vacant. A man Klosterman recognized as Hoyt Vasserman sat in an upholstered rocker by a sheet-iron stove, smoking a cigar and reading a newspaper.

Sliding his gaze around the room, Klosterman decided that Hannabe had to be in one of the rooms in the back. Before moving around to the back, the foreman inspected the horse tethered beside Hannabe's at the hitch rack.

It was a smoke-gray stallion with brown spots on its chest. The foreman's eyes narrowed and his nose wrinkled when he saw the Blacklaws Copper Kettle brand burned into its flank.

"What in tarnation?"

Turning, Klosterman headed back to the cabin's rear. He followed the sound of muffled voices and sighing bedsprings to a window on the far side of the lodge. Removing his hat again, he edged a look between the half-closed curtains.

When he saw Hannabe, he ducked his head with a start. Then he edged another look above the pane.

Hannabe sat in a chair against the wall. There were two people on the bed before him. One was a girl, the other a man whose face Klosterman couldn't see, because the girl— a chubby brunette—was straddling the man, her naked back hiding his face. The girl was bouncing away on the man as though on a Tennessee Thoroughbred heading for the gate. The man's hands kneaded her hips as she worked.

In the chair, his hat on a knee, Hannabe was talking to the man with so little expression that they could have been at a meeting of the Hill County Stockmen's Association. It was almost as though Hannabe wasn't aware of the girl's

presence at all, other than to slide his cold eyes across her
now and then.

But then, the brunette didn't seem to be aware of him
either. At least, he didn't seem to be impeding her perfor-
mance any. Why, if she worked that hard on Klosterman,
she'd probably break something in his old bag of bones. . . .

Klosterman could see Hannabe's lips moving and hear
his voice, but he could make out only occasional words—
not enough to know what the hell the man was talking
about. Then the girl threw her head back with a laugh,
arching her spine over the man's knees, revealing his
hatchet face.

Klosterman's heart thumped so hard he thought it was
going to explode. The man on the bed, under the girl, was
Vince Blacklaws.

Startled, Klosterman ducked his head and stared into the
darkness behind the roadhouse, his thoughts swirling. What
in the hell was an Anchor rider doing with an Anchor enemy like Blacklaws?

Edging another careful look through the window again,
Klosterman saw Blacklaws crawl out of the bed nude and
begin dressing. The girl lay on her right elbow, curling a
finger in her hair, while Hannabe tossed his hat on his chair
and began taking off his clothes.

Nude, his member jutting, he crawled into the bed with
a businesslike air, shoved the girl onto her back, and settled
himself brusquely between her legs. The girl chuckled and
smoothed a lock of hair from Hannabe's eyes. He flicked
her hand away, scolded her, and went to work. The girl
winced, laughed nervously, then lay back against the pillow, turning her head to the side, her features tightening, a
flush rising in her cheeks. Hannabe began pumping his hips,
staring at a knot in the wall above his head.

Blacklaws watched the two, grinning and voicing obser-
vations as he dressed, then settled back in his chair as
though at a dance house or carnival show, hiking a boot on
his knee. When Hannabe was through, he climbed off the
girl and began dressing. Blacklaws grinned, saying something to the girl, who drew the sheet angrily over herself
and turned to face the wall.

When Hannabe had finished dressing, both men tossed several coins on the washstand. Blacklaws bade the girl good-bye, waving his hat at her back, and then he and Hannabe opened the door and walked out, settling their hats on their heads.

Klosterman tightened as he drew away from the window. He'd been so wrapped up in the bizarre happenings inside the room that he'd forgotten his horse. He'd left it on the trail. If Hannabe headed back that way, he's see it for sure.

Turning, Klosterman ran up the grade, casting wary glances behind. When he reached his horse, he untied it from the shrub and led it off the trail about twenty yards, dipping into a shallow, steep-banked ravine. He hadn't moved any too quickly, he saw when he cast another look back at the roadhouse. Both men were riding up the trail, their cantering horses clip-clopping on the well-worn path, their dust billowing in the starlight.

"Damn," he said to himself, wiping the sweat from his forehead, "that was close."

Deciding to follow the unlikely pair and see where they were heading next or maybe pick up some snippets of their conversation—anything to find out what they were doing together—Klosterman mounted up and gigged the pie out of the ravine. He brought the two riders into view about ten minutes later.

He followed at what he thought was a safe distance, heading back the way he and Hannabe had come. But then, after rounding a bend, Klosterman halted the horse and frowned into the darkness ahead.

Hannabe and Blacklaws appeared to have vanished.

Klosterman's heart began hammering when two figures rose up from behind rocks on either side of the trail, starlight winking off rifles in their hands.

"Charlie, what in the hell are you doin' out here this time of the night?" Hannabe asked as he and Blacklaws stepped onto the trail.

Before the old foreman could wrestle his pistol from his holster, the two men raised their rifles to their shoulders and fired.

11

WHEN DOC EVANS had put his horse up at the livery barn earlier that evening, after he, Stillman, and Matt Parrish had returned to town from the Anchor Ranch, he made a beeline for Sam Wa's Café on First Street. He was hungry enough to pad out his belly with an entire buffalo, but guessed he could settle for Sam Wa's liver and onions preceded by a ladle or two of the Chinaman's egg-drop soup.

He was as thirsty as he was hungry, however, and thus considered a shot or two of brandy at the Drovers before dinner. But then he decided to talk Sam Wa's waitress, Evelyn Vincent, into slipping him a shot from Sam's own private reserve, which she had been known to do in the past for Wa's most loyal customer and Evelyn's most generous tipper.

"Oh, no you don't, Doc!" Evans heard to his surprise as he stepped into the small café. The pretty, blond Evelyn Vincent had turned toward him from the counter, where she'd been piling fresh doughnuts on a plate.

"What?" Evans said sheepishly, dropping his gaze to see if he'd tracked horse dung in from the street.

Evelyn shook her head. "I'm under strict orders not to serve you tonight, Doc. Mrs. Kemmett had a feeling you'd come here first thing after returning to town, and she made me promise to send you home. She's got a special supper all planned." Evelyn gave him an elaborate, teasing wink.

Evans frowned, not sure how to take the news. "Oh, she does, does she?"

His relationship with Katherine Kemmett, a minister's widow and midwife who had also been acting as assistant to Evans for nearly a year, was a troubled one at best. Just when Evans had thought they were merely two professionals working together out of the same office—Evans's house—he sensed romantic signals emanating from the woman. But when he'd tried acting on those signals, the signals disappeared like smoke on the wind, and it was back to the whorehouses for Clantick's physician.

Now, it appeared, she was back to sending signals. Evans felt like a stud bull taunted by a cunning, elusive heifer.

"Come on, Doc," Evelyn said with a cajoling smile. "Go on home. It won't hurt you to eat the woman's food."

"Oh, you don't know this woman, my dear," Evans said. "No, no, no—you don't know this woman at all."

Evelyn shrugged. "Seems nice enough to me. A little persnickety maybe, but you don't want to keep frequenting"—she shielded her mouth from the other customers and whispered—"hurdy-gurdy houses all your life."

"Oh, don't I?" Evans said. "Just what's so wrong with hurdy-gurdy houses?" A conversation ceased to his right, and he turned to see two middle-aged ladies in matronly dresses gazing at him under beetled brows.

"No, you don't," Evelyn said, leaving the doughnuts on the counter, marching across the room, and taking his arm. Leading him outside, she said, "Mrs. Kemmett has been all afternoon whipping up an elaborate meal for you, Doc, and whether you like it or not, you're going to eat it. Now go home and enjoy yourself!"

"The women in this town certainly are getting aggressive," Evans carped from the boardwalk.

"It's the push for women's rights. The newspapers have been full of it lately."

"It's a frightening world and getting more frightening every day," Evans grumbled as he donned his bowler. He started down the boardwalk.

Evelyn chuckled. "You have a good time. And no stopping in the Drovers for courage either. I was given orders to see that you headed straight home without delay."

"The woman's a fiend," Evans said with a sigh.

As an afterthought, Evelyn added from the open doorway, "Oh, but you can stop in for breakfast tomorrow, Doc. I'm dying to hear what went on out at the Anchor ranch today!"

Evans waved without turning around and grumbled on down the boardwalk. But he wasn't really as miffed as he appeared. Earlier, when Ben Stillman had mentioned heading home to the supper Fay no doubt had waiting for him, Evans felt a vague pang of loneliness well up from deep beneath his breastbone. He'd imagined a woman in his kitchen and the table all set for supper. At the time, it had been a fanciful image born of vaguely wishful thinking, or so he'd thought. It had, in fact, been real.

There really was a woman cooking supper for him at home—even if it was the most frustratingly complicated woman Evans had ever known but hadn't bedded.

As he climbed the butte to his two-story red house on the west end of Clantick, night shadows gathering around him and the hunger pangs assaulting his ribs, he wondered what it would be like having a woman at home every day, cooking supper for him every night. In the past, he'd always scoffed at marriage, deeming it an institution that kept men bound to watchful eyes and apron strings.

Lately, however—since he'd begun feeling small, erratic flames of warmth for Katherine Kemmett, in fact—he'd wondered if it was time to give up the soiled doves and his excessive drinking and gambling, and settle down to a cozy, domestic life at home with a wife.

After all, everything in life was give-and-take. Give a

little of that, take a little of this. Accept that, refuse the other. . . .

So wrapped up in his thoughts, he hadn't even realized he'd pushed through his front door before he heard, "Oh, hello, Clyde. I see you ran into Evelyn."

Katherine Kemmett stood at the stove, placing a carved oval of dough in the middle of a half-baked pumpkin pie.

She was dressed in a hip-hugging green serge skirt and cream cotton blouse with lace up the front and around the collar, which wrapped neatly around her neck and was fastened with an ivory brooch. She usually wore her chestnut hair in a prim bun atop her head, but tonight she wore it loose, with ringlets dancing about her ears.

Evans had told her once, when he'd had too much to drink and the fires of desire were burning in his loins, that he preferred her hair down as opposed to up, but he hadn't thought she'd been paying attention. Usually when he told her such things, she merely scoffed, shook her head, and changed the subject.

He closed the door gently as he appraised her now, knowing a dull electric charge firing deep within. She looked damn nice tonight. . . . damn nice . . .

"Yes," he said, clearing his throat and gathering his wits, "yes, she caught me. I was about to sit down to some of Sam's liver and onions."

He was thinking that Katherine always looked at least ten years older than her thirty or so years, but tonight she could have passed for her actual age, six or seven years younger than his own thirty-seven. He believed she was even wearing some rouge, or was that a natural flush in her cheeks? And her breasts didn't appear to be all wrapped up and pressed flat against her chest. . . .

"Good," she said as she placed the pie in the oven. "I thought it was high time you had a home-cooked meal."

"You just cooked for me—what was it—two weeks ago?"

"A man needs a home-cooked meal regularly and often. All that café food is hard on the stomach."

She turned to him, setting the leather pads on the counter

by the range. He was regarding her stiffly, not sure what to do. He wanted a drink in the worst way, but he always felt like a criminal when imbibing in her presence.

"How about a drink?" she said with a genuine smile, apparently reading the need in his eyes. "You look like you've had a hard day."

He wasn't sure she wasn't playing with him—she could be as sarcastic as she was patronizing—until she reached into the cabinet over the range and removed a brandy bottle and two snifters. She set the snifters against the wall on the table, which was usually covered with the books he always read while he ate or drank, which were now arranged neatly on the shelf below the clock. She uncorked the bottle and poured two fingers into each.

"There, we'll both have one," she said jovially, as though she'd been drinking all her life. Evans had never seen her drink anything but church wine, and even then she wrinkled her nose.

"You're going to have a drink?"

"Why not?"

"What's the occasion?"

"Oh, I don't see how one could hurt."

"I've been trying to convince you of that for months."

"No, Clyde," she corrected him with an affable smile, "you've been trying to convince me that drinking six or seven couldn't hurt."

He shrugged and pulled a chair out from the table. "Got me there, I s'pose."

"Cheers," she said, lifting her glass.

He chinked his glass against hers and drank, restraining himself from taking the entire shot in one gulp. It had been one hell of a long day and, while he'd been contemplating having a drink and a plate of Sam Wa's famous liver and onions before heading for a whorehouse, he had to admit this was nice.

It was damn cozy, as a matter of fact. Also, it told him that Katherine liked him more than she'd been letting on of late. But if she thought fixing him the occasional meal was going to keep him from sinning with the ladies at Serena's Pleasure Palace, she had another think coming. It would take a hell of a lot more than that to keep him from enjoying his life as a free man.

It would take . . . well, to put it bluntly . . . it would take a little of what he was getting at Serena's.

She must have caught him glancing at her bosom, which was more ample than he'd thought, for a slight flush rose in her cheeks and she leaned over, her arms crossed on the table.

"So, tell me about your day," she said. "How did it go with you and the sheriff out at Anchor?"

Evans tossed the rest of his drink back and held the bottle over her glass, from which she'd taken only one tiny sip. When she waved him off, he refilled his own snifter, set the bottle on the table, and told her about the day.

He found that, while he talked, a warm feeling came over him. He'd rarely discussed the details of his days with anyone, and for that reason they never seemed quite real. There always seemed to be an unsatisfactory, half-lived quality about them. But now, sharing the details with Katherine, he saw the day in a new light. It was as if his experiences seemed more real through his sharing them with someone, this woman who'd prepared his meal in his kitchen.

It was a warm, satisfying feeling. A secure feeling, unlike few he'd ever felt before while sober.

"That's just awful!" Katherine exclaimed when he'd come to the end of his story.

"What?"

"It's just awful if it's true, if Matt Parrish really is innocent and it was one of Tom Suthern's own riders who killed him."

Evans looked at her, vaguely amazed. It did seem awful indeed, and her having had that reaction to his story really made it clear to him. He frowned. "Yes, it is, isn't it?"

He wondered if she'd felt the same way about her days as he now felt about his. As if they only seemed to be truly real and genuinely experienced for having been shared with someone else, if only through the telling.

"It certainly is," Katherine said, taking another small sip

from her glass. "What's going to happen now?"

"I don't know. I guess Ben's going back out there, to talk with each of the Anchor riders individually, see if he can fish out some reason why one might have wanted ol' Tom dead—aside from his being a crotchety son of a bitch, that is." Evans flushed. The curse had slipped out, but Katherine hadn't seemed to notice. At least, she didn't chastise him for his blue tongue, like she usually did.

What had gotten into her? Had she finally realized, as Evans had known all along, that he was the best catch around—despite his blue tongue and dark yearnings?

"Well, I hope the sheriff gets to the bottom of it," Katherine said as she thoughtfully ran a finger around the rim of her snifter. "And I certainly hope Matt isn't the killer. I've heard he has an awful temper, though."

"But not the killing kind," Evans said. "I don't believe that for a minute. The real killer's out at Anchor, I have a pretty strong feeling."

They both considered this for a while. Katherine took another dainty sip of her brandy, and bolted to her feet. "My gosh, I'm gonna burn that stew if I'm not careful!"

She opened the oven and, using hide mitts, removed a covered cast-iron pot. She set it on the stove and lifted the lid. "I hope you're hungry, Clyde. I made a ton."

"I could eat a whole herd of buffalo and go stalking a bear," Evans said, sniffing the aroma wafting from the uncovered kettle. "Good Lord, that smells fine, woman! What you have cooking there anyway?"

"Shepherd's stew," Katherine said, beaming as she removed plates from a cabinet.

"Where'd you get the lamb?"

"Herbert Teal brought three quarters over yesterday—to pay us both for services rendered. Remember those twins we delivered three months ago?"

Evans was pumping wash water at the sink. "Damn near forgot." He chuckled. "Someday I'd like to get paid in real money, but at least we won't starve."

As he splashed water on his face, he stopped, embarrassed, and turned to Katherine, who was ladling the steaming stew onto the plates. Had she noticed his use of "we," as though they were already a couple above and beyond their business relationship? If she had, she wasn't letting on.

Evans finished washing, then took his place at the table. He waited while she removed the biscuits from the oven, knowing she always liked to say grace before eating. The practice annoyed him—he was not a God-fearing man—but after the meal she'd prepared, he guessed he could give her a few seconds of silence.

He did so, and when she'd finished her table prayer, he dug into the stew like a boatman after a long journey up the Mighty Mo.

When they'd finished the main meal, Katherine served up the pumpkin pie and poured coffee. Evans marveled at the dessert. He didn't think he'd ever tasted cobbler so delicious, with such a rich, succulent taste of pumpkin so deftly spiced. Come to think of it, he didn't think he'd tasted home cooking this good since he'd come west from his home in New York City nearly ten years ago. Katherine had really outdone herself this time.

And once again, he couldn't help wondering why. . . .

While she washed the dishes, he sat at the table and poured himself another brandy, amazed that she did not object or even give him one of her vague but nettling reproving glances. He smiled and shook his head and found himself staring at her backside as she worked.

She had one hell of a nice form, he concluded. Hell, she had as nice a form as many of the whores he frequented downtown. Her derriere was nicely rounded, neither too large or too small. Her stomach was flat, her legs long, and her bosom was ample—a couple of handfuls anyway. When she turned to remove a pot or pan from the range, he noticed how her breasts jiggled slightly in her blouse, the nipples making small, barely noticeably protrusions in the cloth.

What he wouldn't give to see this prudish minister's widow in her birthday suit, spread out naked on his bed!

She was nearly finished with the dishes when he stood

and moved to her, feeling a heat in his loins. She was here for a reason, by gum. She'd cooked him this wonderful meal for a reason. Perhaps she intended to stay the night?

Carefully, anxiously, his breath shallow, he put his hands on her shoulders. She froze, her back straight as a broom handle. He too had frozen, standing there with his hands on her shoulders, knowing from past experience that he couldn't get too pushy. He had to find out her intentions before proceeding and possibly ruining the whole evening.

"Clyde," she said, turning to him. She lifted her chin and gazed into his eyes.

He leaned down slowly, waiting for her hands to come up and push him away. They did not, and his lips met hers. They stayed there for several seconds, her lips parting slightly. She tensed, and he pulled away.

She pressed her hands to her apron, drying them, and placed them on his chest, not so much to push him away, it seemed, as to place a subtle barrier between them.

"Clyde," she said again. "Not here."

His mind reeled, hopeful. What was she saying? She'd sleep with him elsewhere? His heart drummed in his chest.

"Where?"

She pondered this, dropping her eyes and swallowing hard. "In a week, I'd like you to come to my place. I'll cook supper for you there." She lifted her chin again and smiled. Her cheeks were flushed and her mouth twitched nervously. "Okay?"

Gravely, trying not to reveal the desire and anticipation surging through him, he nodded.

Then she stood on her toes and kissed him gently on the lips, lightly taking his face in her hands.

"I better go now," she said, pushing past him. Gathering her coat and hat off the rack by the door, she looked at him and smiled. "In one week. Six o'clock. I'll make you a lovely supper."

Evans's lips and mouth were dry. He cleared his throat and nodded. "I'll be there."

"Good-bye," she said.

Finding his voice again with effort, he managed, "Thanks . . . thanks for the wonderful meal, Katherine."

"It was my pleasure, Clyde." She held his gaze for several seconds, smiling, then turned and walked out the door.

Evans stood in the kitchen, hearing her buggy clatter away in the night. His ears rang with hopeful anticipation.

He nodded slowly and grinned. "I'll be goddamned."

12

"HOW'S HE DOING?" Ben Stillman asked Nancy Suthern the next day around noon. She was reentering his office after visiting Matt Parrish in the cell block. Leon McMannigle stepped through the door behind her, the ring of cell keys in his hand.

Nancy shrugged. "As well as can be expected . . . for a man accused of murdering his fiancée's father," she said, crossing her arms over her sheepskin coat.

She wore a simple blouse beneath the coat, and a long, dark wool skirt—a warm outfit for the cool buggy ride to town. She was a pretty girl, but she looked tired, as if she hadn't gotten much sleep last night. Stillman felt deeply sorry for her. Her father was dead and she was left with a run-down ranch, a roll of misfits, and a worthless brother.

Topping it all off, the man she loved and had planned to marry was behind bars. The judge had held the hearing that morning. He'd ordered that Matt be held without bail, and had set a pretrial hearing in two days. The actual trial would follow soon after.

The world was a cold place sometimes. Damn cold. Stillman wished there was something he could do to help

Nancy, but about all he could come up with was to do his damnedest to prove Matt Parrish's innocence. If such a thing were possible, that is.

"I'm sorry, Nancy," Stillman said, perched on a corner of his cluttered desk, a cup of coffee in his hand. "I'm sorry I had to arrest him, but there was no other way."

"I realize you were just doing your job, Sheriff." Removing her brown felt hat from the chair before Stillman's desk, Nancy donned it with a distracted air, as though she hadn't yet digested the tragic events of the past twenty-four hours.

Stillman cleared his throat. "It sure would be helpful if you could think of anyone who might have wanted to see your father dead."

"It wouldn't necessarily have to be anyone who would profit from it money-wise," Leon added, pouring a cup of coffee at the ticking stove. "Might've been someone he had an argument with lately—outside of Matt, of course. Heck, maybe he got into it with a traveling drummer or some out-of-work cowpoke ridin' the grub line."

Nancy sank into the chair before Stillman's desk, her eyes wide and painfully thoughtful. Slowly, she shook her head, regarding each man in turn. "I just can't think of anyone, I'm afraid. I wish I could. I'd like it to be anyone—anyone at all—besides Matt."

"Let me ask you this," Stillman said, wrinkling his brow and regarding her gravely. "Putting your woman's intuition to work for me—forgetting for the moment that you love Matt and plan to marry him—do you think it's at all possible, even remotely possible, that Matt was angry enough with your father to kill him?"

Nancy looked at him sharply, opening her mouth to speak. But then she stopped, reconsidering, and let her eyes roam the room as if looking for the elusive answer to the sheriff's question.

Finally, in a small, unconvincing voice, she said, "No. Matt couldn't do it. I just know he couldn't."

Stillman looked at Leon, who looked back, his brows raised.

"Well, I best be getting back to Anchor," Nancy said, rising from the chair and removing her deer-hide gloves from her coat pockets.

"You mind if I ride with you?" Stillman said. He finished his coffee and set the cup on the desk. "I'd like to have a talk with your men."

"No, of course not," Nancy said. "I'd be happy for the company, as a matter of fact."

Stillman went to the coat tree and shrugged into his buckskin coat and cream, high-crowned Stetson. Moving to the gun rack, from which he plucked his Henry rifle, he said, "Why don't you stay here by the stove while I saddle my horse? I'll come and get you when I'm ready to head out."

"That would be fine, Sheriff," Nancy said, taking her seat once again.

"Here—have a cup of my coffee." Leon poured her a mug. "Best in town."

"If you like it strong enough to melt a mule shoe, that is," Stillman warned the girl as he opened the door and went out.

When they were on the trail, heading south of town, Stillman asked Nancy about her plans now that her father was dead.

"Oh, I intend to hold onto Anchor," she said as though the decision had not been a hard one. "And when you've cleared Matt of the murder and we're married, we'll run it together." She smiled at Stillman bravely.

"Then I guess he'll get what he's after, won't he?" Stillman said with a wry arch of his brow.

Nancy stared over the head of the horse pulling her leather two-seater. Her voice was vaguely troubled and uncertain as she said, "Yes, I guess he will."

They rode quietly after that, Nancy breaking the silence once, to invite Stillman and Fay to her father's funeral, which she'd planned for the next day.

"I doubt there will be much of a crowd," she said. "Dad burned quite a few bridges over the last year or so."

"You'd be surprised how quickly people can forget their

anger when the one they're angry at has passed on."

"Do you think so, Sheriff?" she asked, swinging a look at him.

Stillman nodded. "I think so."

When they came to the Anchor's main gate, Stillman swung down to open it. He stopped suddenly when a rifle cracked in the distance. Another barked, and then another. Several pistol shots followed.

"My God!" Nancy cried. "Those shots are coming from the yard!"

Hurriedly opening the gate, Stillman said, "You wait here, Miss Suthern. I'll ride up to the headquarters and find out what's going on."

He forked leather and gigged Sweets up the trail. The gunfire grew louder and, rounding a bend, he saw puffs of powder smoke rising from the pasture behind the bunkhouse. Men with rifles were shooting from a shallow ravine, toward the ranch yard. Others returned fire from around the outbuildings.

The sporadic but heated volleys sounded like the skirmishes Stillman remembered from the War Between the States.

As he jumped out of the saddle and grabbed his Henry rifle from the boot, a wounded man cried out, shouting epithets.

"I got one!" called a man crouched behind a woodpile at the rear of the blacksmith shop.

A man in the ravine yelled, "Yeah, but you're not long for this world, you son of a bitch!" Then he levered a shell in his rifle breech, laid the barrel on the ravine's grassy lip, and fired. The slug tore into the woodpile as the opposing shooter ducked his head.

Stillman slapped Sweets's rump, frightening the horse out of firing range, then slipped through the barbed-wire fence and hunkered behind the bole of a cottonwood. Gazing toward the yard and the ravine in the foreground, he sized up the situation. In the ravine were several men he recognized as Matt Parrish's Circle P riders.

He levered a shell in the Henry's chamber, then ran

crouching through the brush to the ravine, entering the shallow draw about twenty yards to the left of the closest
shooter.

"Goddamn this week," Stillman groused as he ducked
into the ravine. A bullet spanged off a rock to his right,
and he flung himself against the bank.

"Harry Littleton—is that you over there?" he called to
the Circle P man on his right.

The lean, gray-haired man jerked, startled. Turning to
face Stillman, he said, "Who in the hell is that?" He levered
his carbine and held it up as though preparing to shoot.

"Ben Stillman, Hill County Sheriff!" Stillman called.
"What in the hell do you think you're doing?"

"These men framed our boss for Suthern's murder, Sheriff!"

"Whether they did or they didn't, what you're doing here
is against the law!" Stillman returned, hands cupped around
his mouth. *"Now tell your men to hold their goddamn fire!"*

Scowling, Littleton turned reluctantly to the others lined
out along the ravine. "Hold your fire! Boys, hold your fire!"
he called, cupping his hands around his mouth.

Slowly, the gunfire in the ravine died. The Anchor men
kept shooting for nearly a minute, but they too ceased
shooting, no doubt because the Circle P men had ducked
below the ravine's lip.

"What the hell's going on?" a Circle P rider called to
Littleton.

"This is Ben Stillman," the sheriff called loudly enough
for the Anchor men to hear. "If any of you takes another
shot, you better shoot me, 'cause I'm gonna haul your sorry
ass before the judge!"

"Those hombres started it, Stillman!" an Anchor rider
called. Stillman recognized Otero's Spanish-accented English. "They came in here looking for a fight, and they got
one."

Littleton turned his red face to Stillman. "We just came
over to do a little investigatin' on our own, Sheriff. Just
wanted to look into the killin's all. Ain't no way our boss

killed Suthern." The Circle P foreman shook his head. "Just ain't no way!"

Stillman sighed. He should have known there'd be trouble out here. All the Anchor riders had been at the hearing earlier today, and they'd left town soon after, their jaws jutting like open barn doors.

"A judge and jury will decide that," Stillman called to Littleton and his men. "All you men are doing is causing more trouble and keeping me from getting to the bottom of Suthern's murder. Now, I want you to get your horses and ride on out of here."

"We leave this ravine, they'll backshoot us," the man to Littleton's right exclaimed.

"No, they won't," Stillman promised, making sure his voice carried to the Anchor crew. "Because I'll shoot the first man that fires another shot. You shoot at me, you better make sure your aim's true," he said for the Anchor men's benefit. He doubted they would. Their fight was with Parrish's men. Besides, killing a lawman would only open a new can of worms.

Stillman looked at the Circle P riders, lying or sitting against the ravine's bank, their heads below the lip. They shared sour, uneasy glances.

Stillman climbed out of the ravine and faced the Anchor men. "You boys keep your irons quiet. The Circle P boys were just leaving."

He glanced at the ravine. Finally, a man crawled up the opposite bank, swinging cautious looks behind him. Then another man did the same, clutching his wounded arm. Then another and another climbed out, until all six Circle P men were heading for their horses grazing near some cottonwoods about a hundred yards away.

Stillman faced the Anchor crew, his Henry in the crook of his arm. He found Otero staring at him from behind a hay rake, and he stared back, his features just as cold.

Hearing clomping hooves and rattling wheels, Stillman turned left and saw Nancy Suthern trotting her buggy up the road. She turned off the drive and approached the rear of the bunkhouse. Bringing the roan horse to a stop, she set the brake and stood, gazing around.

"What is going on here?" she asked tensely, directing her question at no one in particular.

The Anchor riders only looked at each other guiltily.

She glanced at Stillman standing thirty yards away. Then she lifted her chin, gazing beyond him at the Circle P riders gathering their horses.

She turned to Otero, who had limped out from behind the hayrick, loosening the thong holding his black hat on his head and holding his Winchester down toward the ground. He grinned sheepishly and shrugged.

"Just a little misunderstanding, Miss Suthern," he said. "The Circle P riders came calling, wanting to know who framed their boss for the murder of your father. I told them they were barking up the wrong tree. One of them pulled a pistol." He shrugged again. "That's what started the whole thing."

Stillman had walked up to the buggy. To Nancy, he said, "Matt's men had their tails twisted, but I doubt they'll be back. They're cowboys, not fighters." He gave Otero a wry glance, and the Mexican grinned.

By now, the other Anchor riders had come out and were gathering behind Otero. Two were missing—the foreman, Charlie Klosterman, and Dave Hannabe. Stillman wondered where they were. Tommy Jr. wasn't here either, but Stillman had heard that the kid rarely worked with his father's crew. He was probably either drinking or sleeping off a drunk.

Her face ashen and her jaw tight, Nancy said, "I will not have any fighting over this matter." She gazed directly at Otero. "Do you understand, Mr. Otero."

"I understand, Señorita, but like I said, it was the Circle P—"

"I know what you said, but it takes two sides to wage war. I will not have my father's memory sullied any more than it already is by a range war. I hope I've made myself clear."

She got down from the buggy, glanced at Stillman, and

turned to her men. "Sheriff Stillman wishes to speak with each of you. I want you to cooperate with him fully. When you're done answering his questions, I want you all to get to work. We have much to do before my father's funeral tomorrow, including the digging of a grave."

She turned to Stillman, who had been watching her admiringly. She appeared to possess more than a little of her old man's grit, which meant she'd probably be all right. "Mr. Stillman," she said with a parting nod.

"Good day, Miss Suthern," he said, pinching his hat brim.

She turned her cool slate-gray eyes on Otero. "Please have my horse and buggy put away." Holding her skirts above her low, black boots, she disappeared around the bunkhouse, heading for the main lodge.

Stillman looked at the Anchor riders. They stood gazing at him snidely, heads canted to one side, chewing tobacco or grass stems or drawing their lips back from their teeth.

Well, this ought to be interesting, he thought.

13

"YOU GOT A hell of a lot of nerve coming back out here, Stillman," Otero said as he hobbled through the bunkhouse door, leaning on a homemade walking stick. He stopped and frowned. "Hey . . . what the hell are you doing?"

Stillman was sitting at the end of a long table, near the range. He had his Colt out, and he was aiming down the barrel, one eye squeezed shut. "I'm wonderin' if I can hit the same spot on your leg I hit yesterday."

Otero jerked, nearly falling with his stick. "What? You're crazy. *Madre Maria,* put that thing away, lawman!"

Stillman squeezed off a shot, the Colt jumping, smoke puffing. Otero jumped to the side as the slug tore into the floor near his right boot. Losing his balance, the Mexican fell awkwardly on his side, tearing several coats from the wall pegs. His cottonwood stick clattered on the puncheons.

"*Madre!* You are a crazy son of a bitch!"

"Yes, I am," Stillman said. "That's what happens when a murder's been committed in my county and I'm having trouble finding the culprit. Now, would you like to pull your mangy carcass over here and have a seat, or should I have another go at that leg?"

He thumbed back the trigger and squeezed his right eye closed.

"No, wait! I'm getting up, I'm getting up!"

While Otero reached for his stick and began climbing to his feet, one of the other cowboys stuck his head through the door tentatively, a wary look on his face.

"You'll be called in due time, Sykes," Stillman told him. "In the meantime, get out!" This wasn't his usual way of questioning witnesses and possible murder suspects, but he was outnumbered out here at Anchor. He figured that showing these waddies what a hardcase he could be might even the odds a little, cause them to think twice before jumping him.

Cursing in Spanish and regarding Stillman with a look of half-rancor and half-diffidence, Otero hobbled over to the table, lifted his good leg over the bench, and sat down, wincing against the pain.

"How's the leg?" Stillman asked as he built a smoke.

"It hurts," Otero growled. "And you had no call. Parrish killed the boss. From where I come from, you kill the man who kills the boss." He gave another Spanish curse and sighed as he set the stick on the bench beside him.

"This isn't where you come from," Stillman said, licking the cigarette paper and folding it closed. "This is my territory, and folks abide by the law here or suffer the consequences." He struck a match against the scarred surface of the table, lit the quirley, and waved out the match. "Tell me what you were doing the night Mr. Suthern was murdered."

"I was loading hay in the barn. I went to the well for some water. I heard the gunshots and ran toward the creek." Otero shrugged, blinking.

"What did you see when you got to the creek?"

"Señor Parrish crouched over Señor Suthern's bloody carcass." Otero's eyes were flat, but a mocking glint had grown in their muddy depths.

"That kind of contradicts your earlier story, doesn't it?"

"Huh?"

"Before, when you were getting ready to lynch Parrish, you said you'd seen him shoot Suthern."

Otero thought about this and rubbed his jaw. "Did I say that? Well, I saw him kneeling over the old man with his Colt still smoking. That's as good as seeing him do it. *Que no?*"

"His revolver was smoking?"

"Sí."

"That's funny," Stillman said. "Suthern was shot with a forty-five-sixty Kennedy carbine rifle." He stared hard at Otero, who flushed and looked away.

Finally, the Mexican said ruefully, "I think you are trying to talk yourself into your friend's innocence, Sheriff."

"Think so?" Stillman had to admit, if only to himself, that he was inwardly pleased with Otero's conflicting stories, but he didn't fool himself into believing it got Parrish off the hook. Otero's lie didn't mean Matt was telling the truth.

"I think so," the Mexican said.

"I'm beginning to think it's just as likely that you did the shooting."

Returning Stillman's gaze with a challenging one of his own, Otero said, "Why would I bite the hand that feeds me?"

Stillman took a deep drag off his quirley. Blowing smoke, he said, "That's what I'd like to know."

Otero only shrugged.

"You and Suthern ever butt heads?"

Otero chuckled. "You butt heads with Mr. Suthern, Señor, and you're drifting real fast. Besides, he paid a fair wage and jobs aren't easy to find for a brown man in white-man country."

"Not even for a gunslick?"

Otero grinned. "Not even for a gunslick."

Stillman studied the coal of his quirley as he flicked ashes on the floor. "Any of the other men lock horns with Suthern? Get fighting mad? Killing mad?"

"None that are still around."

Stillman nodded. "Where are Klosterman and Hannabe? I haven't seen them around today."

"Must be on the range somewhere," Otero said, lifting his hands and dropping them.

Studying Otero through a haze of cigarette smoke, Stillman wondered if the Mexican could have had a stronger motive than Parrish for killing Suthern. He doubted he'd be able to squeeze that information out of him, however.

"Get out of here, Otero," he said, glancing at the door. "Send the next man in. But don't wander far . . . you hear?"

Otero glowered at Stillman, offended. "I do not run from any man, even the legendary Señor Stillman." He grabbed his stick and, sighing painfully, got up, lifted his bad leg over the bench, and hobbled outside.

Over the next hour, Stillman questioned five more men, learning little more than what he'd learned from Otero, and coming up with no viable reason why any of them, including Otero, would have killed their boss.

The last man he talked to was young Andy McKenna. Stillman had nearly wrapped up the conversation when he asked the stocky young wrangler about Klosterman and Hannabe. None of the others had seemed to know where the two men were either.

"They've been gone since last night," the kid said. He spoke in a thick, dull voice, and his wide eyes betrayed his anxiety at having to speak with a lawman. Fidgeting with his weather-beaten hat in his hands, he added, "Late last night, or early this morning. I don't know what time it was."

Stillman had been ready to pack up his cigarette makings and drain his coffee cup, but now he settled back in his spindle-backed chair, regarding young McKenna with interest.

"You mean both men left the ranch in the middle of the night?"

"That's right, sir."

"Together?"

McKenna shook his head. "Nope."

Stillman frowned, trying to keep a rein on his impatience. "Tell me about it, boy."

"Well, sir, I woke myself up last night yellin' for a horse. I do that sometimes—wake myself up like that. Well, when I woke up last night, someone was movin' around in the bunkhouse. Real quiet-like, like they didn't want anyone to know they was up. Well, I just laid there, and pretty soon I seen it was Mr. Klosterman. When he left the bunkhouse, I got up and went to a window to see where he was goin'. I ain't no snoop, ye understand—I was just curious."

"I understand, I understand," Stillman said, nodding for the kid to continue. "What did you see out the window?"

"Well, first I seen Dave Hannabe ride out from the stables. Then, a little while later, here comes ole Mr. Klosterman, ridin' the same way."

"They weren't riding together?"

"Nope," McKenna said. "It sorta looked to me like Mr. Klosterman was followin' Dave sneaky-like, like he was tryin' to find out where Dave was off to without Dave knowin' he was there."

Stillman thought about this, fingering his leather makings pouch. He remembered seeing Klosterman walking near the creek late yesterday afternoon, near where Suthern's body had been found, as though he'd been looking for something.

Finally, Stillman lifted his gaze to McKenna. "Do you have any idea where they were headed?"

"No, sir," the kid said. "I can't figure it. Unless . . ." He seemed reluctant to continue.

"Unless what?"

Young McKenna shrugged. "Well, I shouldn't say, 'cause I don't know an' I don't want to get nobody in trouble. . . ."

Stillman regarded the kid with gravity. "Son, Mr. Suthern was killed. Then two men rode out of here, secret-like, in the middle of the night. Whether or not the information gets anyone in trouble, you need to tell me where you think they were going."

McKenna was staring at his hat in his hands. He was

kneading the brim like it was bread dough. He shrugged his blocky shoulders and said, "I guess . . . well . . . maybe ole Dave was headin' for the roadhouse."

Stillman thought it over, trying to remember any road-houses out here. "You mean Vasserman's place?" he said finally. He'd visited the remote stage stop and roadhouse only once or twice. He'd heard that Vasserman often had whores around, though, and that his place was popular with area cowpokes, when they didn't feel up to the longer ride to Clantick.

"What makes you think that?" Stillman asked.

McKenna shrugged again and shuffled his boots on the floor. "I just can't figure out where else Dave would be headin'. An' I know for a fact he visits the roadhouse now and then." The kid swallowed nervously, flushing slightly as he stared at the floor.

"You have any idea why they aren't back yet?"

"No, sir, I don't."

Stillman believed him. "Thanks, Andy. You can go."

"Thank you, sir," the lad said, standing, donning his hat, and heading quickly for the door, his spurs singing loudly.

Stillman sat there for several minutes, thinking it all through—Suthern's murder and the disappearance of Klosterman and Hannabe. Were the two events part of the same puzzle? If Stillman learned where Klosterman and Hannabe had gone and why, would he be any closer to learning the identity of Suthern's killer?

Finally deciding to check with Nancy before leaving the ranch, Stillman shoved his makings pouch in his shirt pocket, donned his Stetson, and left the bunkhouse. Heading for the main lodge, he saw two men digging a grave on a slight rise behind and to the right of the house. The others worked in the blacksmith shop or stables or tended horses in the corral.

No carriages had been parked before the lodge. It appeared that Nancy Suthern had not had even a single visitor—odd in the wake of a death. At most places under similar circumstances, the yard would have been packed with saddle horses and carriages, and people dressed in their Sunday finest would have been coming and going all day long.

Stepping onto the deserted porch, Stillman knew a pang of sorrow for young Miss Suthern, whose crotchety father had apparently cast himself as well as his family into social exile. And contrary to Stillman's earlier prediction, that exile had continued even after the old man was gone. Tommy's behavior probably hadn't helped any. At least Stillman and Fay would make an appearance at the funeral tomorrow, and he was sure Jody and Crystal would as well.

Nancy answered his knock dressed for ordinary house chores in a blue gingham dress and apron. Her expression was hopeful. "Hello, Sheriff. How did it go?"

"Hard to tell," Stillman said. "I have a question for you, though, Miss Suthern. Do you have any idea where Klosterman and Hannabe are?" He doubted she did, but it couldn't hurt to ask.

She glanced around the yard, frowning. "They aren't here?"

"No. One of the men told me they both left late last night or early this morning, Klosterman after Hannabe."

Nancy frowned. "Whatever for?"

"That's what I'm wondering," Stillman said. "I didn't think you'd know, but I thought I'd give it a shot."

"I certainly don't know, Sheriff. Wherever those men went, it wasn't on my orders. I can't imagine why they haven't returned by now." Nancy looked puzzled as well as worried. "You don't think it has anything with my father's murder, do you?"

"Right now, Miss Suthern, I don't know what to think about anything." He hated to admit it, but it was true. He was pure-dee baffled. "Well, I think I'll take a little ride, see if I can find them. Good day, Miss Suthern."

"Good day, Sheriff. Please let me know what happens, will you? I'm very curious."

"I'll do that," Stillman said, donning his hat as he turned away. He stopped and turned back to her. "Miss Suthern— Nancy," he said, feeling uncomfortable. "Are . . . are you okay? Can I help you with anything?" He wasn't sure what it would be, but she certainly was alone. Her brother was probably off getting drunk in town or had his face buried in a poker hand. Tommy was about as responsible as a fox in a chicken house, and Stillman knew he'd probably be throwing the kid behind bars one of these days—if he could ever pin him to one of the stage holdups that occurred around Clantick two or three times a year, or to one of the bank robberies in the outlying villages.

Stillman's question seemed to have embarrassed Nancy, who blushed slightly and lowered her eyes. "No, I'm fine, Sheriff. Thank you."

"It just seems a shame you're all alone at a time like this."

She smiled bravely. "I'm used to being alone, Mr. Stillman. I started getting used to it a long time ago."

Stillman nodded. No doubt she had, for she'd been the only female on the ranch since her mother died five or six years ago. "Well, if you ever need anything, I or my wife would be happy to help."

"Thank you, Sheriff."

Stillman touched his hat and moved off down the porch to the yard, heading for his horse tethered to the corral. Climbing into the saddle, he glanced at the sky. It was mid-afternoon, and already the autumn light was weakening. It got dark early these days, but he decided he'd probably have enough sun to ride out toward Vasserman's roadhouse and look into what had become of Klosterman and Hannabe.

It was damn strange that they hadn't returned to the ranch by now. The prickling at the back of Stillman's neck told him things were going to get a whole lot stranger around here.

14

STILLMAN PICKED UP two sets of tracks he guessed were about ten hours old a half mile from the Anchor headquarters. Judging from the way the second set of shoe prints obscured the first, indicating that one man was following the other, he figured he was on the trail of Hannabe and Klosterman.

Why the foreman would have been shadowing Hannabe, Stillman had no idea, but he intended to find out. In light of Suthern's murder, the two men's behavior smelled too fishy to be ignored.

Like young Andy McKenna had figured, the tracks led to Vasserman's roadhouse. The sun was angling westward when Stillman reined Sweets into the yard and tied the horse at the hitch rack. A stage had just pulled out, it appeared, as sweat-lathered horses milled in the corral off the barn while a hostler in overalls and floppy hat forked hay into the feeding racks.

As Stillman mounted the stoop, a calico puss meowed from the railing, jumped down, leapt a crate of empty jelly jars, and hightailed it off the porch and around the building. Inside the cabin, the proprietor, Hoyt Vasserman, was clearing one of the recently vacated tables of dirty dishes while a dark-haired girl scrubbed the top of another with a sponge.

Seeing Stillman, Vasserman stopped with an armload. "Well, hello there, Sheriff. Don't see you out this way much." Vasserman was tall and lanky, with gray hair and a spade beard.

"Howdy, Hoyt," Stillman greeted him, removing his hat. "Looks like you got your hands full here . . . literally."

"Business has been picking up since the Injuns settled down. I ain't complainin'."

Stillman nodded and did away with the small talk; it was getting late, and he didn't feel like camping out unless it was absolutely necessary. "Say, you see anything of Charlie Klosterman and Dave Hannabe lately?"

Vasserman didn't say anything. His eyes strayed to the girl, who looked back at him. Then the girl's eyes returned to the table she was scrubbing, and Vasserman's gaze returned to Stillman.

"W-who'd you say?"

"Charlie Klosterman and Dave Hannabe."

Vasserman shrugged and shook his head. "Nope, I ain't seen neither one. Why you lookin' for them anyway—if you don't mind me askin'?"

"I'm not sure," Stillman said, his suspicion aroused by the girl's and Vasserman's unspoken communication. "I'll let you know when I find them."

"You do that." Vasserman nodded nervously, feigning a grin.

Stillman studied the man, puzzled, then turned and headed outside.

He stood on the stoop, snugging his hat on his head. Why had the names of Klosterman and Hannabe evoked such a reaction from Vasserman and the girl? Apparently, the two men had been here—which their tracks had indicated—but Vasserman didn't want Stillman to know. Had the roadhouse proprietor been warned to keep his mouth shut?

If so, why?

Stillman led Sweets to the water trough below the singing windmill, and waited while the horse drew water. When the bay had had its fill, Stillman mounted up and headed around the yard, trying to get a sense of things and to fish around, albeit with an unbaited hook.

He'd stopped by the woodshed when the back door opened. The girl appeared, closing the door behind her. She moved toward Stillman, her gray dress swirling about her legs, her hair blowing about her shoulders. She was an attractive girl, as roadhouse girls went in these parts, but her face expressed little joy.

The girl watched Stillman as she moved to the woodshed. She seemed to have something on her mind. However, she said nothing as she stepped into the lean-to and started gathering logs.

"Hannabe was here last night, wasn't he?" Stillman asked her.

The girl piled several logs on her left arm before she replied, "Tryin' to get me in good and deep, ain't you?"

"Am I?"

"Ain't you?"

"I'm just trying to find Charlie Klosterman and Dave Hannabe."

"Well, good luck."

When she had an armload, she started back to the cabin. She stopped as she passed Stillman, who sensed her urge to speak.

"Oh, hell," she said, eyeing the cabin cautiously. Apparently deciding she wasn't being watched, she glanced at Stillman and said, "I don't know about Klosterman, but Hannabe was here last night. Gave me such a pokin', I'm still sore. Hope the son of a bitch rots in hell."

With that, she started back to the lodge.

Stillman called quietly, "No sign of Klosterman, though, eh?"

She stopped and turned, shaking her head. "Nope. Only—" Her eyes widened with fear. She turned again and headed back to the lodge. "Never mind."

She stepped inside and closed the door behind her.

"What the hell was that all about?" Stillman asked himself.

He rubbed his sunburned cheeks with his thumb and index finger, pondering, trying to puzzle it out. Frustrated, he eyed the sky—about two hours of light left—and reined Sweets into the hills behind the roadhouse, following the return tracks he'd picked up on his way in—two riders followed by one, which meant Hannabe had picked up another rider at the roadhouse. Intending to find out where the pair and Klosterman had gone, Stillman urged the bay along the trail.

Soon the sign became scuffed and difficult to read, and the dying light didn't help. He was following a narrow, meandering cow trail when a horse whinnied to his left. He swung a look that way, and saw a pied gelding standing in a pocket between two buttes, chewing the long grass along a runout spring. Something dangled from the stirrup, but Stillman couldn't make out what it was until he'd ridden several yards toward the horse.

Dangling from the stirrup was a man's leg, the twisted, torn, and bloodied body lying facedown in the grass, thin wisps of gray-brown hair swirling about the bald crown of the man's head. The Anchor brand had been scorched into the pie's flank. Stillman knew who the man was even before he got down and turned him over. Charlie Klosterman's sightless eyes reflected the last rays of the setting sun.

"Damn, Charlie," Stillman said, inspecting the several bullet wounds in the man's chest.

Instinctively, he looked around, fingering the butt of his Colt, but he could tell the horse had dragged Charlie a long ways after the Anchor foreman had been shot out of his saddle and gotten his boot caught in the stirrup. The culprits were no doubt far from here by now.

Culprits: Hannabe and whoever he'd picked up at the roadhouse? Stillman grunted and shook his head. Who the hell else?

Ever the nagging question—why?

Stillman shook his head and frowned at the bloodied

body of the old cowboy. He hadn't known Klosterman well, but he knew his reputation. He'd been a man of hard work and loyalty; not even Suthern's crotchety last days had driven him off. And now he lay dead with three or four bullets in his chest, his clothes dusty and torn.

Why had he been killed? Backing up, why had he been following Hannabe, and who had Hannabe picked up at the roadhouse?

So many questions, and night was falling fast. Knowing he couldn't follow the tracks of the other two riders in the dark, Stillman decided to take Klosterman back to Anchor and head home. He'd be back out here tomorrow for Suthern's funeral, and afterward he'd try to pick up Hannabe's and the mystery rider's tracks again, try to figure out where they'd gone.

The men who'd killed Klosterman more than likely had something to do with Suthern's killing as well. It would be too much of a coincidence not to be true, and Stillman had never believed in coincidence.

No, something was going on out here that involved more than Tom Suthern and Matt Parrish, and Stillman would find out what it was if it was the last thing he did.

When Stillman delivered Klosterman's body to Anchor, he was not surprised to see that the only one upset was Nancy Suthern. The cowboys regarded the dead foreman grimly before two hauled him off his horse and over to the barn, where his body would await a simple pine coffin and a hasty burial behind the house.

It was less than what Klosterman deserved, but probably more than he'd expected.

Stillman questioned the other Anchor riders standing around outside the bunkhouse, their features silhouetted by the open door behind them. A couple wore only long underwear and hats, blankets draped about their shoulders. Several smoked. As Stillman had expected, none offered any information about where Hannabe had gone, what business he might have had in the mountains, or what Klosterman might have suspected.

"This is just awful, Sheriff!" Nancy Suthern exclaimed when Stillman had walked with her back to the house. "I can't imagine why anyone would have killed Charlie."

She wore a wool shawl, holding its frayed ends about her. The sky was clear, the air cold—probably close to freezing.

"You have no idea what Hannabe could have been up to?"

Appearing utterly baffled, she shook her head and wrinkled her eyes.

"I suppose your father never said if he suspected the man of anything?"

"Like rustling?"

Stillman shrugged. He could think of no other reason Hannabe would have been traipsing about the mountains at night . . . at least nothing that would have been worth killing for.

"He didn't say anything to me about it," Nancy said. Obviously, she was shaken. Her father was dead, and a killer was loose in Three-Witch Valley. Suddenly, she jerked a hopeful look at Stillman. "This proves Matt's innocence, doesn't it, Sheriff?"

Stillman glanced across the dark barnyard, at the bunkhouse windows spilling small light squares on the hard ground. "About all it proves is that someone else killed Klosterman. But I'll be looking into it further. Tomorrow, after the funeral, I'll ride out and try to pick up Hannabe's tracks again."

"Do you think Hannabe could have killed my father, Mr. Stillman?"

"According to several of the other men I talked to earlier, he was loading hay in the barn at the time. Of course, if some were in on it, they'd be lying. . . ."

Nancy sighed and looked at the bunkhouse darkly. "Then we'd have an awfully big mess on our hands, wouldn't we?"

Stillman nodded. "If you want to ride to town with me, my wife and I would be glad to put you up for a few nights . . . until I can figure out what's going on out here."

She shook her head. "Thank you, no. I'll be all right. My father has plenty of guns in the house."

Stillman smiled. In many ways, Nancy Suthern reminded him of Fay, pretty and strong. "What time is your father's funeral?"

"Eleven o'clock. I appreciate your coming, Sheriff—you and your wife. You'll probably be the only two from town."

"Oh, I reckon Doc Evans will come," Stillman said, trying to sound encouraging. "Maybe Mrs. Kemmett. I'm sure Jody and Crystal will ride over, them being your neighbors and all."

"Yes, they've always been right neighborly, through thick and thin."

"Well, good night, Miss Suthern. I'll see you tomorrow."

"Oh, you can't go before I've fed you, Sheriff! You must be starving."

"I'm right hungry, I have to admit," Stillman said, grinning ruefully, "but I'd better get home. Fay is no doubt worried, and I'm sure she has a plate ready to warm on the stove. Thanks anyway."

"Good night, Sheriff. Give my love to Matt, will you?"

"I'll do that," Stillman said as he stepped off the porch and started across the yard. A few yards away, he stopped and turned back around. "Say, is your brother home tonight, Miss Suthern?"

Nancy shook her head. "I haven't seen him, Sheriff. But that's nothing out of the ordinary, I'm afraid."

Stillman nodded thoughtfully, then touched his hat and wheeled toward his horse.

"Do you think Tommy Jr. is behind this, Ben?"

Fay was bringing the coffeepot from the range. Stillman sat at their small kitchen table, devouring the stew she'd heated after he'd walked in exhausted, trail-weary, and utterly famished.

Fay had been waiting up for him, reading on the living room divan. As usual after he returned late from stalking owlhoots, she'd run to him, kissed him, and buried her face in his chest as though she hadn't seen him in weeks.

"I don't know, but I wouldn't put anything past him," Stillman said, cutting into the roast on his plate. "And he hasn't been around the ranch, so I haven't had a chance to talk to him yet. You'd think that after his father died, he'd be sticking a little closer to home, to help his sister, if for no other reason."

He forked meat into his mouth and sipped the hot coffee Fay had just poured.

She set the pot on the stove. "He's a bandit, isn't he?"

"I know he's held up a couple stages and an express office or two," Stillman said. "Just haven't been able to prove it."

"But do you actually think he'd kill his father?"

"I really don't know the boy well enough to know what he would or wouldn't do." Stillman talked around a mouthful of beef and potatoes. "But if the old man really cut Tommy out of his will, as rumor has it . . ." Stillman shrugged and swallowed.

Fay stood, arms crossed, beside the range. "Well, what about Hannabe? And . . . and why was Klosterman out following him in the middle of the night? And, for that matter, who did he meet at Vasserman's place?" She shook her head, as perplexed and frustrated as her husband. Fay nearly always got wrapped up in Stillman's more baffling challenges.

Finished with his food, Stillman shoved his plate away and wiped his mouth with a napkin. Chuckling, he shook his head. "Yeah, I tell you what—this one's about as puzzling as any murder I've investigated, and I've been in this business a long time."

"Do you think you'll ever be able to sort it out, Ben?"

Stillman stared at his plate. His eyes were tired, his thick, wavy hair rumpled. Nodding, he said, "Yes," and lifted his chin.

His eyes narrowed as he stared at Fay, a smile crinkling the corners of his mouth, lifting his brushy mustache. Her rich, chocolate hair spilled across her powder-blue wrapper, which displayed the ample swell of her bosom to thrilling effect.

"But right now, just for tonight, I want to let it go."

She moved to him. "You look exhausted."

"That I am," Stillman replied as she wrapped her arms around his head, pressing his face to her bosom. "But I have me something else in mind before I sleep."

He sensed her smile. "Oh, what is that?"

"You'll see," Stillman said, drawing his head back and lifting his hands to her shoulders. Slowly, he slid the wrapper and the straps of her thin chemise down her arms, until her full, pale breasts bobbed free. The pink nipples stiffened under his gaze.

He smiled, eyes burning.

"I guess we could work on that baby some more," she said breathily, kneading the hair behind his ears, then running her hands over the heavy muscles beneath his shoulders.

He buried his face in her breasts, fondling them with his big hands, nuzzling them, inhaling the soft, spring-rain smell of her. Then he stood, picked her up in his arms, and carried her down the hall to their room.

15

"ASHES TO ASHES," the minister said, "dust to dust."

The chill autumn breeze rippling the brim of his black, bullet-crowned hat, the Reverend Edward Winkelman turned to Nancy Suthern.

Dressed in a simple black gown and black shawl, a Bible in her black-gloved hands, she stood amidst the other mourners near the open grave on the rise behind the Anchor lodge. Stillman stood to her right and slightly behind her, but he could see that her eyes were dry. She was holding up well.

She turned to her brother, Tommy Jr., and took the cream Stetson the young man was holding. She stepped up to her father's open grave beside the black mound of soil a couple of Anchor hands had dug out of the earth. She kissed the hat and tossed it into the grave, where it settled atop the pine coffin, which had already been lowered within.

"Good-bye, Daddy," she said so quietly that Stillman could barely hear. He noticed that her voice broke, though. Fay must have noticed it too, because she stepped forward and gently placed her hand on Nancy's arm, just letting the girl know she was here, that she was not alone.

To Stillman and the other mourners, including the Anchor riders gathered in a loose group behind him, the minister said simply, raising his arms, "Go in peace, brothers and sisters, and take the memory of this good man with you . . . and do not forget."

With that, the Anchor men, dressed for the occasion in slightly cleaner garb than usual and looking sheepish and about as comfortable as cats in a room full of rocking chairs, glanced at each other, donned their hats, and headed down the hill toward the yard.

The minister—a tall, slender man in his early thirties whose ginger hair breezed under the brim of his hat—turned to Nancy. With a reassuring smile, he clasped her hands in his. After whispering something Stillman couldn't hear, to which Nancy smiled and nodded gravely, the minister sauntered down the hill toward the house.

Jody and Crystal Harmon and Doc Evans and Katherine Kemmett were the only other mourners, as Stillman had feared. After Stillman and the others had offered Nancy their condolences, and Nancy and Fay strolled together toward the lodge, followed somewhat awkwardly by an obviously bottle-feverish Tommy Jr., Stillman turned to Evans.

"Will you see that Fay makes it home all right, Doc? I'm going to ride farther up the valley."

"Whatever for?" Evans asked, frowning behind his glinting spectacles. Katherine Kemmett stood beside him, a little closer than usual, Stillman noted. Looking prettier than usual too, with her hair fashionably styled—and was that rouge on her cheeks?

"Your guess is as good as mine, Doc."

Katherine said, "We'd be happy to ride back to town with Fay, Sheriff."

"Thanks, Katherine."

Jody and Crystal were standing nearby, Jody holding their blond-headed one-year-old, who was playing with Jody's string tie. "You need any help, Ben?" Jody asked.

Stillman could have used the young man's tracking abilities—Jody knew the mountains as well as any man within a hundred square miles—but he didn't want to take him away from his family. Besides, Stillman didn't know what was waiting for him out there. A premonition told him things could get woolly.

"Thanks, son, but I can handle it. You and Crystal and little William Ben enjoy that lunch down at the lodge. I'll see you later."

Evans cleared his throat. "I'd, uh, offer to ride with you, Ben, but I have a pair of tonsils to remove this afternoon."

Katherine turned to him, chiding, "You removed those tonsils yesterday, Clyde!"

Evans nudged her with his elbow and looked away, color rising in his cheeks.

Stillman chuckled. "Thanks anyway, Doc."

"You be careful, Ben," Crystal said. They were all strolling down the rise toward the lodge. Crystal walked beside Stillman, her arm hooked through his.

"Don't worry about me, young'un," Stillman told her with a reassuring smile, patting her hand.

At the lodge, Stillman kissed Crystal good-bye and broke away from the group, untying Sweets from the hitch rack out front. He was about to poke his boot through the stirrup when Fay stepped out the front door.

"Ben, wait!" she called, heading toward him while lifting the folds of her skirt above her boots. Approaching Stillman, she said, "You aren't going to have a sandwich?"

Stillman shook his head. "I best get moving. I don't know how long tracking Hannabe is going to take."

"Will you be back before dark?"

"I just don't know." Stillman wrapped his arms around her waist. "But don't you worry, Mrs. Stillman."

"Oh, I don't worry anymore," Fay said, moving close and smiling up at him. "If I've learned one thing, it's that you're going to do what you have to and my worrying isn't going to keep you safe. But I also know that I love you, Ben Stillman, and if you get yourself killed, I'll never forgive you."

Stillman chuckled, then bowed his head to kiss Fay's ruby lips.

"Okay, you two—that's enough."

Stillman broke the kiss and turned to the porch, where Crystal stood holding little William Ben, who babbled and pointed a pudgy finger at Stillman. "Not in front of your godson," Crystal added with mock derision.

"Just one more." Fay gave Stillman a quick peck on the lips. Then she turned and headed for the porch.

Mounted and riding across the yard, Stillman waved his hat to the two women on the porch, and to little William Ben, who, now in Fay's arms, stared after him, still babbling and pointing in Stillman's direction.

A few moments later, Stillman was on the trail, heading into the mountains. But the feel of Fay's lips remained on his. And he couldn't help wondering if he would be a father soon, with a little boy like William Ben pointing after him as he rode away.

Stillman had ridden a mile from Anchor when he decided that his time might be put to best use by paying a visit to Leonard Blacklaws's Copper Kettle Ranch. After all, there were only two ranches on this end of Three-Witch Valley, and Hannabe and his cohort obviously hadn't been heading for Anchor. The only other destination out here was the Copper Kettle.

Moreover, the first culprit Stillman had suspected of Tom Suthern's murder—after Matt Parrish, that is—had been Leonard Blacklaws. Or one of Blacklaws's men. He knew Blacklaws's son, Vince, hadn't committed the murder, because he'd still been in town, as Stillman had ordered after his and Parrish's fracas outside the post office.

At least, Stillman thought Vince had been in town. He'd have to ask around, maybe visit the girls at the younger Blacklaws's favorite bordello. . . .

The only other person besides Parrish who had a motive for Suthern's murder was Leonard Blacklaws. Everyone in the Two-Bear Mountains knew Blacklaws had been pining to have all of Three-Witch Valley to himself, ever since he'd run a herd up here from Missouri nearly fifteen years ago.

Stillman followed the wagon road eastward, along Upper Three-Witch Creek, for five miles. Finally, looking above the gold-leafed aspen woods rising on his left, he saw Blacklaws's sprawling ranch house atop an eastern bench, beneath a sheltering, rocky ridge. Below the house was the collection of log shacks and corrals and hay barns—all toy-sized from this distance.

Stillman turned off the main trail and followed a fork of the creek southward through the aspens, in which Black-laws's white-faced herd began appearing, cropping the lush grass along the stream. Stillman stopped to let Sweets drink from a backwater eddy, and turned to his left when he heard the clip-clop of hooves.

A rider appeared, a rifle set across his saddle bows, his dark brow furrowed suspiciously under the brim of his tobacco-colored hat. His tan duster was shit- and grass-stained and peppered with burrs, one large pocket torn.

Hearing more hooves, Stillman looked across the stream, where another rider rode out of the woods. The tall red-headed rider held a rifle butt against his shoulder with one hand, the barrel aimed at Stillman. His freckled face was shaded by the low-canted brim of his Stetson. In the hand holding his reins was also a smoldering cigarette.

Copper Kettle riders.

When they drew close and reined up, staring at Stillman grimly, Stillman said, "Hidy-ho there, amigos," with a wry drag of his voice.

"Shit," the redhead drawled. "Lookee here, Rale—it's Stillman."

"Hi, Danny," Stillman said with a grin. Turning to the other man, he nodded. "Rale. Been a while."

"Too long," Rale said.

Stillman knew Rale was pondering the three years he'd spent at Deer Lodge, courtesy of Stillman, for beating a Chinese gandy dancer nearly to death in White Sulfur Springs, when Stillman was still wearing the tin of a deputy U.S. marshal. The redhead, Danny, was no doubt pondering

the broken nose Stillman had given him six months ago,
when he'd resisted arrest in the Drovers Saloon in Clantick.

Stillman sighed through a smile.

It was a damn small world. Especially for a lawman.
Damn small, and getting smaller every day . . .

"Well, I'd like to hang and around and talk with you
boys, but I've got work to do."

"You're trespassing, Stillman," Rale said, cocking his
carbine and wrinkling his nose. "I should shoot you right
now."

"I'm on official business," Stillman said. "If you want to
hang, go ahead and pull that trigger."

Rale looked at the other man, Danny Patton, who was
walking his horse across the creek. "This sumbitch cost me
two years in Deer Lodge for killin' a Chink."

Patton replied, "Yeah, well, he broke my nose a couple
months ago. Hurt like hell. Cost me a week of work. I still
can't breathe right." The redhead reined up about five yards
to Stillman's right, the barrel of his Colt carbine aimed at
the lawman's side. His dull brown eyes regarded Stillman
with simmering malice.

"You two choirboys are gonna have me tearing up like
a bride's momma," Stillman said. "Now put those guns
away, or I'll take you both to Clantick and throw you in a
cell."

Rale laughed without mirth. "How are you gonna do
that? We got you dead to rights."

"Yeah, you ain't so tough now, Stillman," Patton spat.
He took a deep, thoughtful drag from his quirley. "We
could kill you right here, right now, and no one would be
the wiser."

"Wait," Rale said. "I don't want him to go too quick. I
want to have some fun with the son of a bitch first. Let
him die slow-like."

"You mean torture him some?"

Rale smiled. "Why not?"

"I get to break his nose." Patton looked at Stillman. "You
reach under that coat real slow-like and take your six-

shooter out of its holster, toss it on the ground."

"You go to hell," Stillman said mildly.

Rale sat up straight in his saddle. "I'm warnin' you, sum-bitch."

"I'm warning you, weasel. If you boys don't back off, you'll regret it."

"Like I said," Rale yelled, "we're the ones with the guns in your face, Sheriff!"

Stillman gave Sweets the signal with his left spur, and the horse rose up on its hind legs with a whinny, flailing its front hooves like a boxer's fists. Holding tight to the reins, Stillman shucked his Henry from the boot jutting up from beneath his right thigh. As the horse came down, its front hooves knocking Rale's horse over with a scream, Stillman swung the barrel of his Henry soundly against Patton's face as Patton's rifle barked, grooving the shoulder of Stillman's buckskin. Patton cried out as he toppled side-ways from his skittering mount.

Sweets's front hooves connected with the ground once again, swinging his butt around so that Stillman had a clean look at Rale pinned beneath his screaming bronc. As the bronc awkwardly gained its feet, stirrups flapping like wings, Rale reached for his rifle a few feet away.

Stillman levered a round into the Henry's breech, and fired.

"Ahhh!" Rale screamed as the bullet tore through his hand.

With Rale taken care of for the time being, Stillman reined Sweets toward Patton. On his back in the dirt, the hardcase was clawing his hogleg from its holster. Before he could bring it up, Stillman swung the butt of his Henry like a club, connecting soundly once again with Patton's head. So soundly, in fact, that Patton flew back with a grunt and lay still, out cold. His right temple swelled as though snakebit.

Stillman yanked Sweets around again toward Rale, who was cursing and clutching his wounded right hand to his chest while blood oozed onto his shirt.

"You son of a bitch! Goddamn you! You fuckin' son of a bitch!"

"Watch your language," Stillman said, "or I'll add anti-social behavior to the charge of attempted murder."

16

STILLMAN RODE INTO the Copper Kettle compound and halted his horse before the clapboard house with a wide wraparound porch. A chubby girl with braids and wearing a pink gingham house dress was sweeping around the porch's collection of wicker chairs. Above her, on the porch roof, a short, beefy gent with blond, gray-flecked hair was pounding a nail through a new shake. He wore canvas trousers and a gray work shirt.

"Papa, look," the girl said as she stood holding her broom and staring toward Stillman. Her eyes were not so much surprised as amused.

Above her, the older gent ceased pounding and gave his owly gaze to the yard. His coarse brows furrowed over creased eyes as he regarded the lawman astride the tall bay. His gaze moved to the two men standing sullenly behind the horse, about ten and fifteen feet respectively off the bay's black tail.

Danny Patton's and Rale's wrists were tied together. Rope bound their arms to their sides. The end of the rope was tied to the tail of Stillman's bay, who now turned to regard the sulking, hatless hardcases with nothing less than delight.

Patton and Rale, the very picture of despair, did not look at their boss or even lift their chins. Rale's right hand was wrapped with a bloody cloth. Danny Patton's brick-red forehead was swollen to twice its normal size.

Sweets flicked his tail and returned his gaze forward.

Leonard Blacklaws stared at the cowboys as though he couldn't quite believe what he was seeing. Then a smile broke out on his face and he slid his eyes back to Stillman.

"Well, I'll be goddamned."

Stillman jerked his thumb over his shoulder. "Ran into a couple of your boys along the trail."

"I see that," Blacklaws said with a chuckle, lifting his hammer and sleeving sweat from his brow. "I also see they got the short end of the stick. You taking 'em in, Sheriff?"

Stillman shrugged. "Nah. Don't feel like bothering with them. I think they learned their lesson."

On the porch, the chubby girl giggled.

Blacklaws peered over the roof's edge. "Kayleen, is that you down there."

"Yes, Papa."

"Well, go on inside."

"Yes, Papa," the girl said. Smiling again at the two hard-cases standing behind Stillman's horse, the girl turned and went into the house.

Stillman crawled out of his saddle, removed a folding Barlow knife from his jeans pocket, and cut the rope binding the two drovers' wrists. Then he untied the rope from Sweets's tail and swung it up over the men's heads.

As Stillman wound the rope in a loop over his arm, Blacklaws said, "Rale, Patton—collect your wages from T.J., gather your gear from the bunkhouse, and ride the hell out of here. Don't let me see neither of you in this country again."

"Can I get someone to look at my hand?" Rale asked, squinting up at his boss.

"No," Blacklaws said.

Sourly, Rale started toward the bunkhouse. Patton glared

at Stillman, mumbling something Stillman couldn't hear, then turned and moved heavy-footed after his partner.

Looking up at Blacklaws, Stillman said, "You let them go because they jumped me or because I jumped them?"

Blacklaws shrugged as he crawled to the ladder. "Both."

Stillman dropped his rope in a saddlebag and tied Sweets to the hitching post. Blacklaws descended the ladder and turned to the sheriff moving through the gate in the fence around the neatly trimmed yard. Regarding the porch roof, Stillman said, "Don't you have men who can do that?"

"Sure," Blacklaws said. "But if a man can't shingle his own roof, what good is he?" He turned and walked stiffly up the porch steps. "Come on in and sit a spell," he said without turning his head. "I'll see if I can rustle up a cold beer or two. It's just the hard stuff you're laying off of, if I remember right."

"You got it," Stillman said, following the rancher into the dark, cool house.

In the hall, an elderly woman in a dusting cap was scrubbing the baseboards. Blacklaws asked her to bring two beers to the parlor.

"Yes, sir," the woman replied as Blacklaws passed.

The parlor was comfortably outfitted with a thick rug, damask drapes, and big, heavy chairs. Two divans faced each other across a mahogany coffee table. Between two bay windows, a brass spittoon sat at the foot of a high walnut table upon which perched an extremely well-endowed Brahman bull carved from a stout chunk of roan wood.

"That's teak," Blacklaws said. "My eldest daughter, Bridget, married a senator from Connecticut. They travel the world. She sent me the bull last Christmas from Burma. Had it carved special. Nice, ain't it?"

Stillman smiled at the balls. "Impressive."

"Humbling, I think, is a better description." Blacklaws chuckled, fished two cigars from a silver box on the coffee table, and offered one to Stillman, who declined with a simple wave of his hand. Looking around for a match, Blacklaws said, "Have a seat anywhere."

Stillman chose one of the divans, setting his hat on the coffee table. When Blacklaws had found a match and lighted his cigar, he sat in the other divan, facing Stillman. He threw his arms up onto the divan's back and clamped the cigar in one corner of his mouth while blowing smoke out of the other.

Stillman hadn't seen anyone else in the house besides the maid, but muffled women's voices and ceiling creaks told him he and Blacklaws weren't alone. Rumor had it the rancher's wife was sickly and that the youngest daughter and a niece from Kansas City took care of her. There had been six children; one had died during a July Fourth horse race, and the others except for Kayleen and Vince had long since fled northern Montana for more worldly pursuits.

Stillman hadn't seen Blacklaws in over a year. The man had aged, his face more craggy and drawn, his eyes more sunken, his hair and mustache a little more gray. He wasn't as nattily dressed as usual either. The cigar he was smoking, however, probably cost as much as Stillman made in a week.

"I take it you're here to talk about ol' Tom Suthern," Blacklaws said behind a cloud of thick blue smoke.

Stillman nodded. "That's right."

"You have your man, don't you? Matt Parrish?"

"I don't think he did it," Stillman said. "I think someone just wanted it to look like he did it."

Blacklaws pondered this, smoothing his mustache. "Well, I didn't kill him, if that's what you're thinking."

Blacklaws was about to say something else, but stopped when the maid appeared with a tray, two beers, and two tall glasses. She set the tray on the coffee table, poured the beers into the glasses, asked Blacklaws if there would be anything else, and left, her skirts aswirl.

Blacklaws picked up one of the glasses and handed it to Stillman. Then he picked up the other, sat back in the divan, and sipped the beer, licking foam from his mustache. "I might have killed Suthern a few years ago, but why would I do it now? Hell, he was about to go on his own."

"Maybe you got impatient," Stillman speculated.

Blacklaws chuckled, his once-square shoulders rising and falling. "Hell, I waited nearly sixteen years for that old bastard to kick the bucket!" He took another sip from his beer, shoulders jerking again as he laughed.

Stillman drank and set the glass on the coffee table. "Well, it could be yours now, I reckon. If you made Nancy the right offer. She says she plans to run Anchor herself, but you never know. The right offer might change her mind." Stillman was fishing around for just how eager Blacklaws had been to get rid of Tom Suthern.

"Nah," the rancher said. "Look at me. I'm old and gettin' older every day. I feel it in my bones. Five years ago, yeah, I would have made her an offer." Blacklaws shook his head. "Not now."

"Vince could run the other place," Stillman suggested, trying not to sound too probing.

"No, he couldn't," Blacklaws said with open disgust, drawing his lips back from his teeth. "He couldn't run it right anyway. He's not a bad cowhand, but he doesn't have a mind for the larger picture—herd rotation, water, blood-lines. He also doesn't know much about money. I give him more than he's worth and he spends it all on the whores in Clantick. You should know that, Stillman. You've locked him up enough times for brawling."

Stillman nodded. "He gets a little nasty when drunk and provoked. Does a little provoking of his own too," he added, reflecting on Vince's recent fracas with Matt Parrish.

"You can't have that kind of temperament when you're running a spread of any size. Look what happened to old Tom. There at the end, the only men he could get to work for him were either codgers or owlhoots. A couple were stealing from him."

When Stillman raised a curious eyebrow, Blacklaws spoke over the rim of his beer glass. "They were collaring his beef. I seen tracks when I was crossing his spread one day."

"Ever see the cattle or the men moving them?"

"No, but they were being moved, all right. I saw horse tracks too. Sometimes three, maybe four riders."

"How do you know they were Anchor men?"

Blacklaws shrugged. "I don't for sure. But it makes sense. I haven't seen any other riders out this way, and his own men would be the last he'd suspect, wouldn't they? Besides that, there'd be nothing he could do about it, as old an' stove-up as he was." The rancher shook his head grimly. "That's what happens to us. We get old and crippled and the wolf pups take control. I'd just like to know what in hell is going to happen to this place when I'm gone."

Blacklaws glanced around the room with eyes so melancholy that Stillman felt a pang of pity for him. Nonetheless, he said, "Where were you the night Suthern was shot?"

Blacklaws's gaze strayed back to Stillman and acquired a wry cast. He sighed and threw an arm on the divan back. "Let's see, when was that again?"

"Day before yesterday."

Blacklaws pointed at the rafters. "I was on the roof, replacing old shakes."

Stillman scrutinized the rancher skeptically, but his gut told him Blacklaws was telling the truth. It was the rustling that had piqued his interest now. He'd suspected that that was what Hannabe had been up to. Something told him the rustling was connected to Suthern's murder. Admittedly, Matt Parrish was hotheaded, but Stillman couldn't bring himself to believe that the young rancher was capable of cold-blooded murder.

Stillman would give the valley a thorough sniffing before heading back to town, even if it took him a day or two.

He threw back his beer and set the glass on the table. "Thanks for your time, Mr. Blacklaws."

"What? You're leaving?" The rancher looked genuinely dispirited. He was a lonely old man, not all that different from his nemesis, Tom Suthern. "How 'bout another beer?"

"I'd love one but I'd better ride." Stillman pushed himself up from the divan and scooped his Stetson off the table.

"I s'pose you do at that," Blacklaws grumbled, pulling at his mustache. "Stop back anytime. You and me, Stillman—I sense we're cut from the same cloth. We should spend an afternoon palavering."

"I'd like that," Stillman said, extending his hand, which Blacklaws shook. "Thanks for the beer."

Stillman headed for the door, Blacklaws following and making small talk about the weather and the approaching winter. At the door, Stillman turned to him. "Your son around? I'd like to talk to him."

Blacklaws scowled and said with alarm, "You think Vince might have killed Suthern?"

"At the moment, I suspect everybody," Stillman said. He already knew that Vince had been in town—or should have been in town when Suthern was killed. He wanted to check it out with Vince himself.

Blacklaws thought for a moment and nodded, troubled . . . worried. "Well, I seen Vince ride west a while ago. He was probably goin' up to help some of the men cut wood on Blue Mountain."

"I'll be riding that way. Maybe I'll run into him."

Stillman donned his hat, bade the rancher good day, and headed out. As he left the yard, he tipped his hat to Rale and Patton, who were grimly saddling two horses by the barn. Seeing Stillman, Rale lifted his bandaged right hand, sending Stillman a vulgar gesture.

Stillman smiled and heeled Sweets into a trot.

17

VINCE BLACKLAWS HALTED his roan stallion on the ridge above the Anchor headquarters. His deep-sunk, pale-gray eyes slitted with a grin.

All the mourners had left the house. No carriages or saddle horses remained at the hitch rack. Or maybe no one had come. Who in the hell would come to the old bastard's funeral anyway?

Blacklaws's eyes slid to the fresh grave on the knoll behind the house, marked by a simple wood cross. His grin widened. He chuckled, then returned his gaze to the ranch yard.

He was behind the house, but he still had a good view of the yard, and he saw none of the Anchor riders. They were probably out working the range.

Which meant Nancy was in that big, empty house—alone.

Tipping his hat brim over his eyes, he spurred the roan down the ridge, through scattered aspens and shrubs, and bottomed out near a woodshed. He halted his horse and scanned the area. Certain none of the Anchor riders were present, he gigged the roan to the shed, dismounted, and tethered the horse to a metal ring in the shed's double doors.

Hand on his holstered pistol, he stole across the yard to the lodge's kitchen door and pressed his back to the wall as he listened for sounds within the house. Hearing nothing, he tried the doorknob. It turned. Blacklaws shoved the door open slowly, sliding his gaze around the vacant kitchen.

His sneering grin gave his savage features an even more savage dimension, deep lines spoking his eyes.

Bringing his boots down softly on the hardwood floor, Blacklaws moved through the kitchen to the living room. Seeing no one, he crept down a short hall to the uncarpeted stairs, looking this way and that and grinning, like a kid playing an especially thrilling game of hide-and-seek.

He shot a cautious glance up the stairs. The coast clear, he put a hand on the banister and climbed, carefully lifting his feet. Gaining the top, he stopped and listened.

Was that water splashing down the hall on his left?

Biting his lower lip with concentration, he stole down the corridor, taking exaggerated steps on his boot toes.

The sound of gently splashing water grew louder. As he approached a door on his right, he stopped. The door was cracked. Blacklaws leaned forward, peering through the crack.

A few feet before the door, beside a canopied bed, sat a big copper tub. Inside the tub, her back to Blacklaws, sat Nancy Suthern. She was soaking in water up to her neck. Her flaxen hair was coiled atop her head and fastened with a bone barrette.

Oh, what a fine long neck . . .

Oh, what slender, delicate shoulders . . .

A board beneath Blacklaws's left boot squawked. Nancy turned her head.

"Is someone there?"

Blacklaws shoved the door open with a single thrust of his right arm, took one step into the room, and stood there, shoulders square, brows beetled over his leering eyes.

"Hello, Miss Nancy. Came to pay my respects."

Nancy turned full around, her blue eyes widening,

splashing water as she crossed her arms over her breasts. *"You!"*

Blacklaws chuckled, showing his big, square teeth. Her skin was so pale and delicate, her bones so fragile.

"What are you doing here? What do you want?"

"What do you think I want? I want what I seen down at the swimming hole the other day."

"What . . . what are you talking about? My God, you're mad."

Blacklaws threw his head back, chuckling.

"Get out!"

His chuckles grew louder.

"I'll call for my men if you don't leave this instant!"

"Go ahead," Blacklaws said. "I don't think they'll hear you. I didn't see any in the yard. In the meantime, stand up."

Nancy's face flushed and her eyes wrinkled fearfully. "I won't."

"Yes, you will," Blacklaws told her. "You'll stand and give me a close-up look at those nice teats of yours. And then you'll spread yourself out on the bed for me. 'Cause if you don't"—he drew the Colt from the holster on his right hip and spun the cylinder—"I'll start shootin', and I'm a damn good shot."

Nancy set her jaw and narrowed her eyes. Goose pimples appeared on her shoulders and slender arms. "You're an animal."

Blacklaws clicked back the hammer of his Colt. "Stand up."

Nancy's chest rose and fell. She glared at Blacklaws. Finally, she sighed. "Well, I guess I don't have a choice, do I?"

Blacklaws's voice rose from deep in his throat, a lusty purr. "You sure as hell don't."

Slowly, reluctantly, Nancy stood, concealing her breasts with her arms, the water rippling off her body. Blacklaws stared at her concave belly, full hips tapering to slender thighs. A faint, heart-shaped birthmark appeared just below her belly button. Between her elbows, Blacklaws spotted the creamy smoothness of her breasts.

His bright, roving eyes hardened. Color rose in his cheeks. He swallowed.

"Lower your arms."

Nancy was staring at the floor. She sighed and lowered her arms, revealing full, pendulous breasts.

"There," he said after a long time. "That wasn't so hard, now was it?"

Blacklaws holstered his pistol and moved to her.

He stopped a few inches away. Her eyes had been downcast, but now they lifted to his. Suddenly, the fear left them. Slowly, a smile lit her eyes. She threw her arms around Blacklaws's neck and kissed him hungrily.

"Oh, Vince," she said. "I've been so lonesome!"

Laughing, Blacklaws bent down and picked her up in his arms. Water rolled off her feet, splashing the floor. Cackling like a warlock, Blacklaws swung her around in a circle, then carried her to the bed.

"No, Vince," Nancy objected. "Not here."

Blacklaws stopped and frowned down at her. "Where then?"

She placed her hands on both sides of his savage face, kissed him gently, then regarded him with a dark, lusty gaze. Her voice rose barely above a whisper. "I want you to take me in my father's room this time."

Blacklaws just stared at her. Then he threw his head back, laughing, and carried her through the door. "Whatever you say, girl! Whatever you say!"

Later, Nancy Suthern and Vince Blacklaws snuggled together in old Tom Suthern's bed, surrounded by the old man's rustic chairs and trophy heads and oval-framed daguerreotypes of long-dead family members Nancy had never met. On the floor sprawled a bear rug from the grizzly Suthern had shot when he'd first come to the Two-Bears from Ohio.

A fire crackled in the stove. That and the recent coupling had warmed the room enough that Nancy and Vince did not need a quilt. Covers thrown back, Nancy lay atop Blacklaws, her chin on his chest, her hands on his shoulders, which were rounded with muscle and pale as flour.

Blacklaws's big, brown hands kneaded her taut, well-rounded ass as he sucked on a cigar and stared at the ceiling. He was nude except for his thin, red socks bunched around his ankles and from which a couple toes protruded.

"Cobwebs in the ceiling," Vince said absently around his cigar.

Nancy was in a half-doze. "Huh?"

"There's cobwebs in the ceiling. Never seen so many in a house. Barn, but not in a house."

"Since when did you become so particular?" Nancy asked, running her left hand down his right arm, fingering several knotted scars.

"Just never seen so many cobwebs in a house is all."

"Well, he never let me clean in here." She turned her head to look at Blacklaws's face. Half sarcastic, half coquettish, she said, "You worried I'm not going to keep a nice house for you, Vince?"

Blacklaws smiled. "Nah, I reckon you'll do okay. You keep screwin' like you been screwin', you can grow all the cobwebs you want." He cackled and squeezed her buttocks.

"Ow!" she said. "That hurts, Vince!"

He released her. "Sorry."

"Do you have to be so rough?"

"I said I was sorry."

Nancy returned her cheek to his chest. "Sometimes you remind me of him—loud and ill-mannered."

Blacklaws chuckled and chewed his cigar. "Sorry you had to take care of him yourself. When we figured on my baitin' Parrish into a temper tantrum in town, I reckon we never figured on Stillman holdin' me there."

"It worked out all right," Nancy said, tracing a circle on Blacklaws's breast. "I didn't mind shooting him. I enjoyed it."

Blacklaws's looked at her and removed the cigar from his mouth. "Really?"

Nancy smiled wanly and shook her head. "He kept me

tied down here for so many years . . . ordering me around. Treating me like a slave. Laughing when I complained."

"I thought you went away some years back," Blacklaws said.

"I did. Before Momma died, I went to school in St. Louis. But after a year, when Momma died, he made me come back, and I've been here ever since . . . waiting on him hand and foot, enduring his cruelty. By rights, I should've ended up like Tommy."

"Then you would've gotten yourself written out of the will."

"That's right," she said. She lifted her head and gazed into Blacklaws's eyes. "But I held on. I endured for as long as I could. In a few years, after I've gotten the ranch back on its feet, I'll be rich—we'll be rich—and we'll go away together every winter. New York, Santa Fe . . ."

Blacklaws shrugged. "I still say if you'd waited another six months, he would've gave up the ghost on his own."

Nancy shook her head, removed the cigar from Blacklaws's mouth, took a puff, and made a face. With a cough, she gave the stogie back to Blacklaws and said, "I was tired of waiting. I swear the old bastard was bound and determined to live another ten years!" She swallowed and made another face. "Those are awful."

Blacklaws studied the cigar. "I been smokin' these since I was fourteen years old."

"Oh, yeah?" she said, reaching down for his member. "What else you been doing since you were fourteen, Vince?"

Blacklaws grinned. "You sure ain't the kind of girl I used to think you were."

"What kind of girl did you think I was?" She squeezed.

"Hell, I thought you was all starch and crinoline. Sure enough. Pretty as a kitten, but when I seen you at church or in town, I thought, 'There goes Miss High-and-Mighty, too good for nobody. Too educated an' proper for her own damn good.' Then that day I stumbled on you swimmin' in your secret hole . . ." He let the sentence trail off, shaking his head.

Her voice was lusty and seductive as her hand worked on his stiffening organ. "Then you found out how proper I was—didn't you, Vince?"

Blacklaws's face slackened as he stared at the ceiling. His voice was thick with contained passion. "Yeah, I never been so mauled in my life. Figured you was gonna wear it out." He chuckled, then his eyes went dreamy again.

"I might just yet," she said.

He placed his hand on her shoulder, urging her head down. "That's what I had in mind."

"Wait," she said. "What are we gonna do about Tommy?"

Blacklaws looked at her and shrugged. "That's up to you, ain't it? He's your brother."

She thought about it. Finally: "I think we better kill him. I thought it might be best to wait a few months, so no one got suspicious and tied his death to Dad's, but I think he could be trouble. He's been grumbling about wanting a piece of the ranch."

"Your old man wrote him out of the will, right? It's all ours—yours and mine." Blacklaws grinned and stroked her hair. "After we're married, that is. Parrish'll be in jail, and the whole west end of the valley will be ours."

"And after your father's dead, the whole Three-Witch— every square acre—will be ours."

"That's right. And he ain't long for this world, not with that cancer he's got in him."

"I don't know, though, Vince," Nancy said, her eyes growing dark. "Tommy scares me."

"Okay, I'll kill him."

"When?"

Blacklaws shrugged. "Tomorrow, if you want."

"I want," she said, nodding.

Blacklaws nudged her head down. "Now then . . ."

"Wait. One more thing."

Blacklaws sighed. "What?"

"Do you have any idea who killed Charlie Kolsterman?"

Blacklaws stared at her for a second. He frowned. "What happened to Klosterman?"

"Someone shot him the day after I killed Dad. Stillman found him southeast of here. He thinks he was trailing Hannabe."

"Who's Hannabe?"

"One of my father's worthless riders."

"Don't know that one."

"Then I reckon you don't know where he's off to?"

Blacklaws lifted his hands. "How would I?"

Nancy nodded. "I didn't think you would. I was just checking." She thought for a moment. "Funny, though. Damn funny."

"Stillman still poking around?"

"He's back out where he found Klosterman, looking for Hannabe." A smile widened her mouth. "He thinks there's some connection between Hannabe's disappearance and Dad's murder."

"Well, that works well for us, don't it?"

"Good enough, I guess, but I wish he'd just decide Matt did the killing and leave me alone. He makes me nervous."

"He will, sooner or later." Blacklaws blew a smoke ring at the ceiling. "Everyone knows what a temper Parrish has."

Nancy chuckled huskily.

"What's so funny?"

"He wants me so bad, Matt does. And my ranch."

Blacklaws studied her, furrows growing in the bridge of his nose. "You ain't havin' second thoughts about marryin' him, are ye?"

"Hell, no. He never would have gotten Anchor away from my father. He might have a temper, but he's too civil business-wise." She smiled. "Besides, he'll be in Deer Lodge for the rest of his life, if he doesn't hang."

Blacklaws looked mildly indignant. "You might have said it was me you really loved."

"Oh, I do, Vince! I do!"

Blacklaws recognized sarcasm when he heard it. "Yeah, yeah," he said, giving her head a firm shove toward his swollen organ.

Giggling, Nancy lowered her head.

After a while, Blacklaws forgot his indignation. His cigar went out. With an ethereal sigh, he said, "Yep, you ain't near as prim and proper as I once thought you were. No, siree . . ."

18

STILLMAN DISMOUNTED HIS horse and hunkered down on his haunches. He touched his gloved fingers to the track of a cloven hoof amidst the fallen autumn leaves.

Cattle had recently been moved through these woods—ten or twelve head. That wouldn't have been odd if it had been earlier in the year, but by now most of the cattle should have been moved to the lower winter pastures.

Most legitimate cattle, that is.

Stillman looked around at the trees, the sandstone knob lifting on his right, and the natural levee over which the cattle had been driven.

It was about five in the afternoon, and the light was going fast, the temperature dropping.

Stillman climbed into the leather and followed the tracks over the levee, through a ravine, over a saddle, and along a creek curling through a draw. The slope on his left was knee-high tawny grass; the other was pines with a few box elders and aspens mixed in.

The breeze was tinged with smoke.

Stillman followed the creek until he heard the lowing of

restless cattle. Dismounting, he led Sweets up the slope and tied him to a tree, out of sight from the trail. He retrieved his field glasses from his saddlebags, shucked his Henry from its boot, levered a shell in the chamber, then off-cocked the hammer.

Holding the sixteen-shooter in the crook of his arm, he moved along the side of the slope, following a game trail spotted with deer scat, stepping as quietly as possible amidst the fallen pine cones, needles, and branches.

Continuing several more yards, he watched Vasserman's roadhouse take shape at the base of the slope, in a bend of the meandering creek. Smoke whipped from the narrow tin chimney. In one of the nearby corrals, a dozen or so cows bawled as a man took an iron from the fire and touched it to a steer's flank while another man with a rope held its nose taut to a snubbing post. As far as Stillman could see, there were four men in the pen with the cattle.

They were rustlers doctoring brands with running irons. Later they'd sell the beef to a dogieman—a small, hapless rancher—or to some other sucker who didn't know he was buying stolen beef.

It was a profitable game if you didn't get caught, and in this vast land, where rustlers and other owlhoots were a dime a dozen and lawmen few and far between, it was a safe bet you wouldn't get caught.

Stillman stepped out from behind the tree and descended the hill, keeping the cabin between himself and the cattle pen.

He was within twenty yards of the cabin when a cacophony rose around him—a loud, tinny racket that ground his jaws together and made his heart beat like a war drum.

Looking down, he saw the twine he'd just kicked, and cursed. The rustlers had apparently surrounded the roadhouse yard with a trip wire to which they'd attached cowbells.

Son of a bitch!

Before Stillman could move, a voice behind him said, "Don't move, Sheriff." Stillman turned his head and saw Hoyt Vasserman standing in the cabin doorway, wearing a white apron and holding a long, double-barreled shotgun, its barrels level with Stillman's head.

The men in the corral had heard the cowbells and come running. Seeing Stillman frozen by Vasserman's shotgun, they slowed up and came on at a walk, pistols in their hands. Dave Hannabe was the first to approach Stillman.

"Drop the rifle," he ordered mildly.

Stillman considered his play. He might be able to get one or two of the rustlers with the Henry, but the other two and Vasserman would cut him in half. He was probably dead anyway, but there was no use in hurrying things. "I'd just as soon set it down, if you don't mind. Dropping it might foul up the action."

"Well, do it."

Stillman bent his knees, crouching, and set the Henry in the dirt. Inwardly, he cursed himself for his carelessness. He should have known Vasserman had thrown in with these rustlers, offering his corral for a cut of the profits. Stillman was outnumbered here, but if he'd gone back to Clantick for a posse, the rustlers and their cattle would likely have disappeared by the time he'd returned.

Rustlers were like phantoms. They worked quickly and vanished.

Hannabe told Stillman to drop his revolver and cartridge belt. Knowing he had no choice, the sheriff reluctantly complied.

"Now why don't you tell me what in the hell you're doin' here," Hannabe demanded, his cocked pistol aimed at Stillman's belly. His high-crowned Stetson shaded his unshaven face and bushy mustache, and his curly hair fell to his shoulders. His polka-dot bandanna fluttered in the breeze.

"Just came to find out who killed Charlie Klosterman, and why." Stillman glanced at the corral, where the small branding fire crackled, black smoke ribboning, and the cattle bawled. The stench of burnt hair hung in the air. "Now I guess I know. He was onto your little rustling operation. Those are Anchor brands you're doctoring, aren't they?"

"So what if they are?"

"Suthern get onto you too? That why you killed him?"

"I didn't kill Suthern," Hannabe said with a smile.

Stillman watched the man for a while, then started laughing.

"What's so damn funny?"

"Nothing," Stillman said. "I just figured it out is all." His face sobering, he studied Hannabe again and the faces of the three other men flanking him, all dressed in dusty drovers' garb, all holding pistols aimed at Stillman. He didn't recognize any of the others. Had one of these been the man Hannabe had met at the roadhouse last night?

"I don't know what in hell you think you figured, Stillman," one of the men behind Hannabe said, "but you're a dead man." The tall, flat-faced cowpoke stomped toward Stillman and raised his Smith & Wesson.

"Wait, Clayton," Hannabe snapped. "We hear what Vince says about this."

Stillman frowned. "Vince?"

"Shut up," Hannabe said. Scowling, he closed the gap between him and Stillman. "Go to the house."

"Vince Blacklaws?" Stillman asked, perplexed. Were Blacklaws and Hannabe in this together?

Hannabe grabbed Stillman's shoulder. "Move!"

Stiffly, Stillman walked toward the roadhouse. Vasserman stood before him, rifle extended. As Stillman approached, the roadhouse proprietor stepped back inside the lodge's shadows, keeping the shotgun trained on Stillman's waist.

As Stillman stepped inside the building, he stopped and slammed the door in Hannabe's face. Lunging forward, he kicked Vasserman's shotgun, blowing out a window, and grabbed it. Vasserman's grip was tighter than Stillman had expected, however; wrestling over the gun, the two men tumbled over a table.

Just as Stillman wrenched the shotgun from Vasserman's hands and swung it around toward Hannabe, Stillman saw the cowboy swing his arm, gun extended. The .45 connected soundly with Stillman's temple.

The sheriff was out before his head hit the floor.

• • •

In his cell behind Stillman's office in Clantick, Matt Parrish was peeing into a white porcelain thunder mug. When he finished, he set the pot on the floor and buttoned his pants.

"Okay," Parrish mumbled to himself as he stepped to the door. "Here we go."

Parrish buttoned his trousers and stepped to the door. Gripping the flat iron straps, he called for Leon Mc-Mannigle. He'd called several times before a key sounded in the stout wood door to the cell block.

When the door opened, it was not the deputy who peered around it, but the short, gaunt, bewhiskered visage of Banner Harlow in a red-checked mackinaw and black wool cap. Driven nearly mad by loneliness, the old farmer had sold his farm after his beloved wife had recently died, and moved to town. He swamped saloons and worked at Auld's Livery Barn, and occasionally acted as jailer when Stillman and McMannigle were away from the office.

"What is it, Matt?" Banner called.

"Banner?" Parrish said. "Where's Leon?"

"Makin' his rounds. I'm watchin' over the place. What do you need?"

Parrish grimaced. Damn. Why did Banner have to be on duty today? He considered delaying the execution of his plan—he didn't want to hurt the old farmer—but no, it had to be done.

"My thunder mug's full and stinking to high heaven. Will you take it out and empty it?"

Wisps of gray hair poking out from under his cap, Harlow shook his head. "Leon told me not to come back here unless there's a fire."

"Come on, Banner," Parrish pleaded, "the pot *stinks*."

"I can't empty it, Matt. I'm sorry."

Parrish sighed. Hating himself for his treachery but knowing no other way, he said, "Banner, you've known me a long time. You knew my dad and mom. Are you going to tell me you're going to make me sit here and smell my own damn slop all morning?"

Banner stared at Parrish, his eyes troubled and thoughtful. "Well, dangblastit, Leon told me not to come back here, Matt!"

His hope flagging, Parrish beseeched the old farmer desperately. "And under most circumstances, I'd agree. A cutthroat might try to make a move on you. But you know I'm no cutthroat, Banner."

Harlow sighed and set his jaw. "Confound it, Matt, I just can't do it."

"All right, Banner," Parrish said, genuinely crestfallen. "I understand."

Grimly frustrated, Harlow returned to the office, locking the cell block door behind him.

Parrish sat on the cot, the metal supports creaking beneath him. He lowered his head and ran his hands through his hair in frustration.

He raised his head quickly when he heard the key again. The cell block door opened and Banner appeared, face flushed with annoyance. "All right, all right—I'll empty your blasted pee pot!" the farmer grumbled, stomping along the cell block, his heavy boots clomping on the boards.

Parrish smiled as the old man turned the key in the lock of his cell door.

"But you dang well better not tell Leon," Banner said, his eyes flashing angrily.

"I won't, I won't, Banner," Parrish said. "Thanks."

As he stepped through the drawers and ambled over to pick up Parrish's slop bucket, Banner said, "If he or Ben finds out I been back here, much less opened your cell, why, they'd—"

The old farmer stopped and turned, frowning. Faster than Harlow was able to comprehend, Parrish had grabbed the key ring from his hand, stepped through the open door, and closed the door behind him. Locked inside the cell, Banner stared aghast at Parrish through the bars.

"Wh-what on earth . . . ?"

"Sorry, Banner, but there's just no other way," Parrish said, for a second regarding the old man sympathetically. But he couldn't spend another hour in this cell—not with a killer on the loose and Nancy out at Anchor with her father's renegades, any one of whom might have killed old Tom. The thought had shot his nerves.

As Parrish turned and started for the cell block door, Banner Harlow cried, "Matt Parrish, you come back here! Why you . . . you come back you ring-tailed walabagoose!"

"Leon'll let you out," Parrish called as he opened the cell block door.

"I trusted you, dagnabit!" Banner cried. Then, his tone bereaved: "I trusted you."

Parrish opened the door. Turning to Harlow, he said, "I'm real sorry, old-timer. I'll make it up to you later. I promise."

He stepped through the door and closed it, hearing Banner rage, "You two-faced snake, why, when I get my hands on you—!"

Parrish didn't hear the rest of it. He was too busy opening and closing the drawers of Stillman's desk, looking for his gun and cartridge belt. When he found them, he wrapped the belt around his waist and peered out the window, looking up and down the street. Not seeing Leon, he opened the office door and stepped onto the boardwalk.

A tall Appaloosa stood across the street, before the tinware shop. Looking around self-consciously, hoping no one noticed him, Parrish marched across the street and unhitched the horse from the rack.

Quickly, he threw the reins around the horn and climbed into the saddle.

"Matt?" a startled voice sounded to his right. "Parrish, where do you think you're goin' with my horse?"

Turning to the man standing in the door of the tinware shop holding a burlap bag at his side, Parrish said, "Sorry, Alvin. I'll have the horse back to town as soon as I can."

Before Alvin had time to reply, Parrish had jerked the horse around and was galloping eastward in a flurry of hooves and dust.

At the edge of town he turned south, heading for the mountains.

19 .

LEON MCMANNIGLE HAD just stepped out of the barbershop, where he'd stopped for a trim while making his regular rounds, when he heard a commotion on First Street, across from the jailhouse. Looking that way as he donned his black Stetson, he saw several men had gathered before the hitch rack outside the tinware shop. They talked loudly and jerked angry gazes eastward up First Street. One of the men, whom Leon recognized as Alvin Anderson, who cut wood for Fort Assiniboine, seemed to be making most of the noise.

On the other side of the street Bill Sunday, who owned the tinware shop, stepped out of the jailhouse and yelled to the others, "Ben ain't in and neither is Leon."

"Great! Just great!" Anderson cried. "That jasper run off with my best horse!"

Leon stepped off the boardwalk and angled eastward across the street, wondering what all the ruckus was about.

"Wait a minute—there's Leon!" Bill Sunday said, pointing.

The others jerked their gazes toward the deputy. Alvin

Anderson ran to meet him. "Leon, that damn Matt Parrish stole my horse!"

Stopping in the middle of the street, McMannigle turned to the flushed woodcutter who wore a duck-billed watch cap and high-topped boots. His blue eyes were capped with snow-white brows.

"Parrish?" Leon said, incredulous. "What are you talkin' about? Matt's behind bars."

"No, he ain't," Anderson said, wagging his head. "He cut out of your office and took my Appy! Lit outta town like the hounds o' hell were on his heels."

His blood racing, McMannigle swung around and started toward the jailhouse. Bill Sunday was still standing on the stoop. He stepped aside, looking both wary and excited, as McMannigle turned into the office.

"Banner?" Leon called, swinging his gaze around the room and hoping like hell Alvin Anderson had been imagining things and that Matt Parrish was in his cell. Seeing that the old farmer was not in the office, McMannigle cursed and headed for the desk. He was opening the drawer in which the key usually stayed when he heard a muffled voice call his name.

The voice seemed to be coming from the cell block.

Leon saw that the key ring was on the desk instead of inside. Grabbing it, he moved quickly to the cell block door, cursing when he found it unlocked, and stepped through.

"Banner?"

"Leon, let me outta here! Matt, he tricked me, that no-good rascal of a ring-tailed varmint!"

Sure enough, Banner Harlow was standing inside Matt Parrish's cell, peering flushed and wide-eyed toward Leon, his hands gripping the iron straps until his knuckles shone white. Parrish was gone.

"Banner, what the hell happened?" Leon asked as he stuck the key in the lock.

The old farmer's face crumpled with indignation and woe. "Ah, Leon, I'm sorry!"

"What happened?" the deputy urged again as he threw open the door.

Harlow was so overwrought, he could barely find the words. "Matt, he said he only wanted me to empty his pee pot, and I didn't want to do it, but then I felt bad, and—"

"You opened the door."

"Yep."

"And went inside."

"Sure enough, I did! And before I knew it, he grabbed the keys out of my hand, ran out, and locked the blame door on me!"

Banner shook his head, furious with himself. "You and Ben told me over and over to only come back here in an emergency, and what do I go and do?"

Putting a calming hand on Harlow's shoulder, Mc-Mannigle gazed down into the old man's stricken eyes. Harlow felt so bad about his mistake that sympathy blunted the deputy's anger. "Did Matt give you any hint about where he was going?"

Harlow contritely shook his head.

McMannigle patted his shoulder. "Ease up on yourself, Banner. These things happen." Then he turned and hurried back into the office.

Alvin Anderson and Bill Sunday were waiting for him. "What the hell happened?" Sunday asked. Several other townsmen were peering anxiously through the jailhouse door.

"What's it look like? He broke jail," McMannigle groused as he unlocked the chain over the gun rack.

"How in the hell did that happen?" Anderson snapped.

McMannigle chose not to answer the question. No use embarrassing poor Banner more than he already was.

Grabbing his Spencer repeater off the rack, he swung around to Anderson and Sunday. "Which way did Parrish ride?"

"East down First, then south," Sunday said.

"How long ago?"

"Not more than ten minutes," Anderson contributed.

Leon thought it over as he loaded the Spencer. Parrish

was no doubt heading for the mountains. Why he'd decided to make a break for it, the deputy had no idea—Parrish hadn't seemed that desperate—but he aimed to find out.

"You men move along," McMannigle ordered as he shoved the shell box in his coat pocket. "I'll get your horse back, Alvin. Maybe you can borrow another one to see you home."

When the two men had left, grumbling, McMannigle grabbed his saddlebags and saddle. Heading for the door, he looked behind him and saw old Harlow standing in the open cell block door, looking sheepish.

Fashioning a reassuring smile, he said, "Banner, you man the store while I track Parrish. Consider yourself deputized."

Harlow's eyes lifted, acquired a skeptical cast. "You . . . you still trust me?"

"Of course I still trust you," the deputy said. "Hell, I've tumbled for a prisoner's tricks a time or two myself. You had no reason not to trust Matt. He's a friend of ours."

Harlow stared at McMannigle, confidence growing in his washed-out eyes.

"Man the store, Deputy. I'll see you soon."

McMannigle gave Harlow a parting nod, then turned and jogged toward the livery stable.

"You got it, Leon," Harlow said, his eyes regaining their confidence. He wiped his mouth with his hand, strode slowly toward the desk, and sat down in the swivel chair. His upper lip curled as his anger returned. "That humpbacked son of a gun!"

Gradually, Stillman felt himself rising from a deep, black pit of cold tar. When his head broke the surface, he opened his eyes, blinking several times, regaining his focus. His cheeks rose as he winced against the railroad spike someone had hammered through his head.

Finally, his vision cleared, and he saw that he was inside Vasserman's roadhouse. He was sitting in a chair, his hands tied behind his back so tightly that they at once felt numb and sore and twice their normal size. His feet were tied too.

The tethers and the pain in his head weren't all that made him uncomfortable. Looking down, he saw that his chair had been tipped back against the wall, so that if he tried to get away, the men in the room would hear the chair hit the floor. It was an awkward, off-balance position, and Stillman didn't like it.

But then again, he could be dead. He was mildly surprised he wasn't toe-down in a shallow grave.

Peering through the pain-fog hovering over his eyes, he gazed about the room. Several of Blacklaws's Copper Kettle men were sitting around a long table, drinking coffee and smoking; some were playing desultory games of cards.

Hannabe and Vasserman were sitting in rocking chairs in the corner to Stillman's right. Both men were reading newspapers; Hannabe smoked a cigar. His hat sat on the floor beside his chair.

From the smell, Stillman could tell someone was cooking back in the kitchen. Only a couple of men at the table were talking. They all looked at once anxious and bored.

"Hey, Clement," Hannabe said suddenly, lowering his newspaper. "What time you got?"

One of the men at the table fished a pocket watch from his jeans and flipped the lid. "Dang near five-thirty."

"You boys better go on home," Hannabe said, "so old Blacklaws don't get suspicious. Make sure you haul that wood back, so he thinks you were busy cuttin' all day. Don't tarry along the trail neither."

"What about him?" Clement said, glancing at Stillman.

"Me and Hoyt'll watch him till Blacklaws gets here. We'll decide what to do with him then."

Vasserman turned to Hannabe. "What about the cattle?"

"When did you say the Fogarty boys were coming for them?"

"Day after tomorrow," Vasserman said.

"We'll keep them right here till then."

"I don't like it," Vasserman complained his forehead creasing with anxiety. Tipping his head toward Stillman, he continued. "What if his deputy comes snoopin' around after him and finds the cows?"

Hannabe shrugged casually. "Then we kill him." To the other men, Hannabe said, "Go on home, boys. And don't forget that wood."

Stillman's face was tilted back in the shadows against the wall, so the others couldn't see his eyes. Furtively, pretending he was still unconscious so as not to draw attention to himself, he watched the drovers rise from the table and stomp to the door and outside. In a few moments, they were gone, the hooves of their galloping mounts receding in the distance.

Wincing slightly against the pain in his hands, Stillman wriggled his wrists, trying to loosen the taut ties.

"Well, you're awake," Hannabe said suddenly.

Tensing, Stillman turned to the hairy drover. "Hell of a game you're into, Dave. How long you think you can keep playin'?"

"Long enough," Hannabe said, puffing his cigar. He smiled. "I reckon you ain't in no shape to stop me."

Stillman felt a wave of dread, knowing the outlaw was right. Stillman had walked right into this hog wallow like a damn tinhorn. He deserved whatever Hannabe had in store for him. But Fay didn't deserve to be a widow. . . .

Stillman went back to work, furtively trying to loosen his ties. He doubted he'd be able to get himself free, but he had nothing to lose.

Something sounded outside, and the nervous Vasserman jumped to his feet and hurried to a window. "Horse and rider," he said, reaching for the shotgun propped below the window. He stared out the window several more seconds; then the shotgun sagged in his arms. "Blacklaws."

Hannabe had climbed out of his rocker and was heading for the door. " 'Bout goddamn time."

He opened the door as Blacklaws mounted the stoop.

"Where in the hell you been?" Hannabe asked.

"Got held up at Anchor," the tall, blond Blacklaws said with a grin. His clothes were coated with trail dust. "I came on when I heard ole Stillman's prowling this side of the Three-Witch. Seen anything of him?"

"Who in the hell you think that is over there?" Hannabe

said, flicking a thumb to indicate the lawman in the chair against the wall.

Blacklaws stepped into the roadhouse and turned, his lips stretching a grin. "Well, well."

"I'd tip my hat to you, Vince," Stillman said wryly, "only it's over yonder on the floor."

Blacklaws chuckled and turned to Hannabe. "How come he's still alive?"

Hannabe shrugged and slouched onto a bench, running a hand through his hair. "I wanted to hear what you thought."

"What do you mean 'what I thought'? We sure as hell can't let him go, can we?" Blacklaws chuckled without mirth. "Hell, he's onto us, Dave!"

"You kill him then."

"Oh, that's it." Blacklaws's deep-sunk hawk's eyes flashed shrewdly. "You want me to do it. You want me to be the one to kill the great Ben Stillman."

"No, I'll do it," Hannabe said, indignant. "I just wanted you to be in on the decision, that's all, so if we got caught you couldn't say it was all my idea."

"Okay, okay," Blacklaws said, "it's *our* idea. Now kill him."

Vasserman's girl stepped out from the kitchen, carrying a coffeepot. She regarded Blacklaws with a bashful, co-quettish smile, obviously pleased to see him, and set the coffeepot on the long table before Hannabe, whom she did not regard at all.

"I heard you come in, Vince, and just thought you might like some coffee," she said, smoothing her skirt about her full hips. Stillman had heard she was Vasserman's niece, raised in the Nevada gold camps. Cooking and whoring for Vasserman was probably a step up for her.

"Hi, Angie," Blacklaws said, grinning lustily. "How you been?"

"Oh, for Christsakes!" Hannabe complained.

Blacklaws turned to him, frowning. "What the hell's the matter with you?" He glanced at Stillman. "Kill him and our problem's solved."

Blacklaws turned back to the girl, his lusty grin returning. "Miss Angie, you got a minute?"

The girl smiled and shyly patted her dress flat to her thighs. "For you, Vince, I got two."

Vasserman was still standing by the window. To the girl, he said with stern authority, "You got supper on the stove, missy?"

Blacklaws and the girl ignored the question. Blacklaws crooked his arm. "Well, come on then."

Smiling up at Blacklaws with the proverbial hearts in her eyes, Angie hooked her arm through that of Blacklaws, who led her through a door at the cabin's rear.

"Vince, how in the hell can you think of that now?" Hannabe yelled.

Blacklaws answered by slamming the door. From behind the door came the girl's muffled laugh.

Stillman was working as inconspicuously as possible on the ties binding his wrists. "Well, I guess it's all up to you, Dave," he told Hannabe. "That's quite the partner you have."

"Shut up," Hannabe said. He got up from the bench and walked over to Stillman, drawing his Colt from his holster.

"Better take me outside," Stillman said. "Might get blood on the floor."

"I don't give a shit about blood on the floor," Hannabe grumbled. But his expression of consternation betrayed his reluctance to kill Stillman.

He'd probably never killed a lawman before, but he knew what would happen to him if he got caught. He was probably also thinking about how complicated his and Blacklaws's rustling operation had suddenly become. Soon there would be three murders in less than a week. All for a few goddamn cows . . .

Mexico was probably looking pretty good to Hannabe about now.

Nevertheless, he lifted his Colt and spun the cylinder, his gaze meeting Stillman's darkly.

20

"HOW 'BOUT A smoke first?" Stillman said.

He could hear Blacklaws and the girl laughing in the other room. He thought that if he could have just a few more minutes, he might be able to pry his wrists apart.

He wasn't sure what he'd do after that, with his ankles still tied. He wouldn't have time to untie them and attack Hannabe before Hannabe shot him, but he'd do everything he could to stay alive.

Hannabe stared at Stillman, considering the request. Finally, he gave a chuckle and nodded. "Why not? You ain't goin' anywhere."

"My makings are in my shirt pocket."

"Have one on me," Hannabe said. Holstering his pistol, he sat down at the table, produced a small leather pouch from his vest pocket, and began building a smoke.

"So tell me," Stillman said conversationally as he covertly worked his wrists apart, finally feeling a little slack in the rope, "how long you and Blacklaws been stealing from Suthern?"

Hannabe didn't say anything, but he grinned as he sprinkled tobacco on the wheat paper he held between two fingers of his right hand.

"Can't hurt to satisfy my curiosity, can it?" Stillman prodded him. "Like you said, I'm not goin' anywhere."

"No, you ain't," the cowboy allowed. He sighed as he rolled the paper around the tobacco. " 'Bout two months."

"You probably need the money, but what's Blacklaws's reason?"

"Ruin the Sutherns—what do you think? Then, when his old man's dead, the whole damn valley'll be his . . . and mine."

Hannabe smiled, self-satisfied, as he stuck the quirley in his mouth, struck a match on the table, and lit it. He got up lazily, sauntered over to Stillman, and brusquely poked the cigarette between the sheriff's lips.

"Much obliged," Stillman said, puffing on the quirley. While he worked his wrists back and forth against the faintly slackening rope, he rolled the cigarette to the side of his mouth. "Nancy killed her father so she and Blacklaws could inherit her ranch—once they're married, that is, and after Matt Parrish has hung for the murder or been sentenced to life in the territorial pen, freeing up his ranch as well."

Hannabe was sitting at the table again, his arms crossed before him, studying Stillman with interest. "How in the hell did you find all that out?"

Stillman hadn't been sure his theory was right, but he could tell by Hannabe's reaction that it was. "I found a tally book in Charlie Klosterman's saddlebags. He kept his cattle tallies on one side of the page and a sketchy diary on the other. He mentions finding fresh women's shoe prints in the field near where Suthern was killed. It was his last entry. Before that, he mentions seeing Nancy and Vince Blacklaws together in a little glen along Upper Three-Witch Creek."

"No shit?" Hannabe grunted with surprise. "I didn't know the old coot could write."

"He must have been hoping he was wrong, and that the rustling had something to do with the reason Suthern was killed. But he wasn't wrong. Nancy doesn't know you and Vince were stealing her old man's cows, though, does she? She doesn't know you're in cahoots with Blacklaws to steal her herd little by little, and turn her belly-up, with no alternative but to sell Anchor—for whatever she could get for it."

Stillman paused. Hannabe was grinning at him.

Stillman continued. "She thinks she's in cahoots with Blacklaws alone in the murder of her hateful old father, who never would have sold his ranch to Matt Parrish."

"That's why she had no intention of marryin' Parrish," Hannabe said. "I see why you're so damn famous, Stillman. You're a canny son of a bitch. Hard way for you to go out, all strapped into a chair like that."

Stillman ignored the remark as he toiled at his tethers, trying to keep his shoulders from moving and giving himself away. "How come Vince is so certain his old man's ready to kick the bucket? I visited Blacklaws earlier today. He's moving a little slower, but he appears to have at least another ten years in him."

"Cancer," Hannabe said, rubbing his right hand in a circular motion across his gut. "Bellyful."

Stillman nodded as he puffed the cigarette, feeling a moment of regret. He'd found he'd rather taken to old Blacklaws, as he'd sensed Blacklaws had taken to him.

He had the rope loose enough that the circulation had returned to his hands. The rush of blood was painful, and he hoped the discomfort did not register on his face. He puffed again on the cigarette, taking the smoke deep into his lungs, to distract himself from the raw burning in his knuckles and fingers.

If he could only get the rope loose enough to slip a hand free . . .

Meanwhile, the bed squawked in the bedroom, and the girl and Blacklaws grunted and sighed as they toiled together. Vasserman sat in his rocking chair, frowning at the closed door and grumbling that supper was going to be late.

"Another thing I'd like to know," Stillman continued prodding Hannabe, buying time as well as information, "is who else at Anchor is in cahoots with you and Blacklaws, and who else is in cahoots with Nancy."

Before Hannabe could answer, the front door flew open and banged against the wall. Stillman jerked with a start, as did Hannabe, whipping his head around.

"Good question, Sheriff," Nancy Suthern said as she stomped into the room behind Dom Otero, who leveled a shotgun at Hannabe, a fierce light in his mud-black eyes.

Nancy, dressed in a flat-brimmed Stetson, flannel shirt, vest, and tight whipcord trousers, held a .38 Colt in her gloved right hand. "Keep them covered, Dom," she snapped as she stomped to the bedroom door, her boots pounding the floorboards. She flung the door open and bolted inside. Stillman couldn't see her, but above the whore's scream he heard her yell, "Forget the gun, Vince. You move one more inch toward that Colt, I'll blow a hole through your cheating heart. Get up—*both of you*!"

"N-Nancy, we ain't dressed," Vince protested.

"Get up!"

"All right, all right." Stillman heard bedsprings quake and groan. The whore sobbed. Blacklaws said, "Let me grab my jeans."

A gun popped. The whore screamed again.

Nancy said, "Leave them. Both of you get out there!"

"Nancy, what are you doin'?" Blacklaws asked, fear straining his voice. "Nancy, give me that gun or I'll—"

"Or you'll what?" Nancy laughed without mirth. "I've a mind to shoot you right now for stealing my cattle and diddling this whore behind my back! I had a feeling when you left my place earlier that you were up to no good. Just a feeling." She cackled like a witch, causing the hair at the back of Stillman's neck to stand up. Otero held his shotgun on Hannabe and Vasserman, who stood frozen, listening to the commotion in the bedroom but staring back at Otero. A humorous glint shone in the Mexican's eyes.

Nancy's rage continued, barely contained. "We were going to get married, eh? Soon we'd have all three ranches, eh? In the meantime, you were trying to ruin me by stealing my cattle. A few here, a few there, so I wouldn't know three quarters of my herd was missing till the next roundup."

The tirade was punctuated with another pistol shot. All the men in the main room, including Otero and Stillman, jerked with a start.

"No!" the whore screamed. "Vince, get her out of here!"

"Nancy, don't!" Blacklaws pleaded. "Put that gun down and listen to some sense!"

"Get into the other room!" Nancy yelled, squeezing off another round. "I'm never late with Dad's old thirty-eight!"

The whore screamed, outraged. Blacklaws cursed angrily. Bare feet slapped the floor.

Then Blacklaws, tall and pale, his face and lower arms sun-browned, appeared nude in the bedroom doorway. His long, blond hair was mussed, pasted against his forehead. Looking at once exasperated, sheepish, and spooked, he glanced around the main room, his eyes quickly discovering Otero and the Mexican's silver-mounted Greener.

Otero's face spread into a grin, and Blacklaws crossed his hands over his privates. The whore, Angie, stumbled into him from behind, pushing him into the main room. And then Nancy Suthern appeared in the bedroom doorway, her .38 trained on Blacklaws and the girl.

She indicated the table with the Colt. "Get over there and sit down."

Turning to her, flushed with fear, the salt having been scared out of him, Blacklaws said, "Nancy, please. At least let me get some clothes on!"

"Sit down before I shoot your noodle off," was Nancy's firm, quiet reply.

When Blacklaws and the girl had taken a seat at the table, sitting several feet apart, the girl hunched over her breasts and sobbing angrily into her hands, Nancy regarded Hannabe. The Anchor man automatically lifted his arms in supplication.

"Please, Miss Suthern, I—"

"Shut up."

"I just wanted—"

"I said shut up, or I'll shoot you now."

Hannabe slumped to the bench, at the other end of the table from Blacklaws and the girl, and fell silent. Regarding Vasserman, who stood with his hands raised before the window, Nancy said, "What do you have to say for yourself, mister?"

Vasserman returned her stare, his long, horsey face betraying his mortification. Sweat beaded his forehead, and his shoulders bobbed with his labored breathing.

He swallowed. "Listen," he tried, his voice quaking. "I just . . . I just followed Blacklaws and Hannabe's lead. I just needed the money." He paused to swallow again, his breath rushing harder, his face turning redder. "I didn't know who they were gettin' the cattle from. It ain't easy runnin' a roadhouse out here, ye know . . . with a stage only once or twice a week . . . damn owlhoots behind every rock and pine." He was almost crying.

"No, it isn't easy," Nancy said grimly, her face expressionless. "Nothing's easy, though, is it, Mr. Vasserman? It isn't easy being the daughter of the most hated man in the valley either. Living poor because your father can't manage his funds or his men, and living isolated because if you left, he'd cut you out of his will." Her lips stretched a grimace. "Because he needed you."

She paused again, then swung her look to Blacklaws, and then to Hannabe. "And it isn't easy being lied to by everyone at the same time, being made a fool of by men who claimed to want you . . . need you."

Her hands steadied the Colt's barrel, the butt firmly ensconced in her unshaking fist, the bore turned toward Hannabe. Still working on freeing his wrists, feeling hopeful as he pulled more and more slack from the rope, Stillman tightened his jaws as he waited for Nancy's .38 to bark, blowing a hole through Hannabe and another through Blacklaws.

And then she'd turn the gun on the girl and Vasserman.

And then she'd shoot Stillman too, because he knew it all, had heard and seen it all.

"Please, Miss Suthern," Vasserman pleaded, his voice breaking. "Please . . ."

"Don't worry, I'm not going to kill you."

Otero looked at her, his eyes vaguely curious.

"Yet," she added for the Mexican's benefit. "Not here."

"Where then?" Otero asked her.

Delaying her answer, she looked at Stillman. So far, she'd only glanced at him once or twice. Now she said, "So now you know it all, Sheriff?" She offered a chill smile.

"I reckon I know it all," Stillman acknowledged with a grim nod. Just then, he wriggled his right hand out from under the loop that had bound it to the left. He kept both hands behind his back, waiting for the right time to make his move.

Her eyes returning to Otero, Nancy said, "We'll take them all to the south end of the valley. I don't want to kill them here. I don't want their bodies found. It has to remain a mystery, so their deaths can never be tied to us—or to my father's murder."

A low groan rumbled up from Otero's throat. "I say we kill them now—make it look like they killed each other. Go on home."

"No, we do it my way, Dom," Nancy said, moving toward the Mexican, her long, slender legs moving gracefully as she held the revolver on Blacklaws, smiling at him. "I don't want anything to intrude upon our venture, yours and mine."

With that, she slid her eyes from Blacklaws to Otero, wrapped her left arm around the Mexican's neck, and kissed him hungrily.

"Well, I'll be goddamned," Stillman almost said aloud.

He wondered who was the biggest fool around here—her, Blacklaws, Hannabe, or Stillman himself. He guessed he was, since he'd ridden headlong into this mess and never would have figured Nancy Suthern for pairing up with the likes of Dom Otero. He guessed it got mighty lonely out there at Anchor for a young woman of marrying age. And for a woman of Nancy's obvious desires, determination, and ruthlessness.

Stillman wondered if she'd ever loved either of them,

Blacklaws or Otero. Nah. A woman like that didn't know love. Love had been wrung out of her by her father a long, long time ago. Or maybe she'd never been born with any in the first place.

All Stillman knew was that, whatever her reasons, she was just as evil as any of the others in this room. And that she'd kill him, Stillman, just as dead as she'd killed her father.

Unless he could somehow get the jump on her and Otero . . .

21

"EVERYONE OUTSIDE," NANCY ordered, gesturing with her Winchester's barrel.

"Where we going?" Hannabe asked.

"You'll see soon enough. Out!"

The naked Blacklaws was still covering himself at the table. In the wake of Nancy's kissing Otero, however, he'd been staring at the Mexican with bald hate in his eyes.

Turning to him, Nancy said, "What's the matter, Vince? Did you think I should have been as loyal to you as you were to me?"

Blacklaws slid his hateful stare from the Mexican to Nancy as she continued. "I knew about your reputation for whores, and I wasn't stupid enough to believe that just because you were diddling me you'd stop diddling *them*. Besides," she added, glancing at Otero, "Dom and I have been enjoying each other's company since the very first night he rode onto the Anchor compound looking for a job. Dom knows how to appreciate a lady, don't you, Dom?"

Otero was grinning, his muddy eyes slitted. *"Sí, señorita!"*

Nancy chuckled as she returned Otero's lusty gaze. Turnng back to Blacklaws, she said, "Get outside. Now."

Blacklaws's expression turned indignant. "Wh-what are you talkin' about? It's gettin' dark and cold, and I ain't dressed."

"I said get outside," Nancy ordered through gritted teeth, shoving the barrel of her .38 into Blacklaws's face.

Slowly, he stood. It was an awkward maneuver as he covered himself with his hands. Nancy stepped around him, prodded his back with the rifle, and then watched, smiling with amusement as he followed Otero to the door, his bare feet padding along the floorboards, hands crossed over his genitals.

When all three men—Hannabe, Blacklaws, and Vasserman—were outside, Otero went out too. Inside the cabin, Nancy turned to the girl, sobbing at the table while hunched over her breasts, hair hanging in her face.

"I'll teach you to frolick with my men, you common harlot," Nancy said.

Nancy grabbed the girl's hair and pulled her out of her chair. The girl shrieked angrily, cursed, and ran out the door, covering her breasts with her hands. In the doorway, Nancy stopped and called to Otero, "Get them all on horses. We're riding to Witch's Butte."

"Witch's Butte?" Otero called back, incredulity in his voice. "That's a two-hour ride from here."

"Just get them on their horses, Dom, and tie them to their saddles."

She turned to Stillman, who held his loose hands together behind his back. He was glad Otero was outside. He thought he could take Nancy alone. If he could get the revolver away from her . . .

Nancy grabbed a bread knife off the table and walked toward Stillman, gazing at him with a peculiar light in her pretty, evil eyes.

"Well, well, just you and me," she said.

"Yep, here we are."

She stopped before him, feet spread, and stared down into his face. Her flaxen hair framed her cheeks.

"You'll have to die, just like the others," she said. "It's a pity too. I kind of liked you."

"I'm a right likeable fella," Stillman wryly allowed.

"You and I, we might have had a time of it," Nancy said, her voice softly husky, her eyes staring seductively into his. "Would you have liked that?"

"I'm a happily married man."

"Yes, I've seen your wife. She's lovely. But I bet I could have enticed you."

Stillman shook his head. "Doubt it."

She placed her gloved left hand on his cheek. "My, you are a handsome piece of maleness. Strong, but I bet you can be passionate too, can't you? They don't make them like you anymore."

"I reckon they broke the mold after me."

She threw her shoulders back, thrusting her breasts out taut against her flannel shirt. "When you rode out here earlier, I was thinking of luring you into my bedroom. Now, that would have been a much nicer way to spend the day, don't you think?"

Stillman stared up at her dispassionately. "I'd have to think it over."

Her expression hardened as color rose in her cheeks. Suddenly, she slapped him hard across the face. "You bastard!" she cried.

She'd brought her hand back to slap him again when Stillman grabbed the .38 with his left hand. Bringing the chair down on the floor with a loud thump, he bolted to his feet, bulling into her, knocking her flat on her back and falling on top of her. His movements were constrained by his tied ankles, but he looked around for the bread knife he'd heard clatter to the floor while at the same time keeping Nancy pinned with his body.

Addlepated, she groaned and struggled against him without heat.

Clutching the revolver in his left hand, he flailed around with his right until he felt the knife. Grabbing it, he reached down to cut his ankles. When they were free, he grabbed the .38 in both hands and was about to stand when, looking up, he saw the silver-plated butt of a shotgun plunging toward his face.

The next thing he knew, the cold, black tar was consuming him once again.

McMannigle was about five miles south of Clantick, rounding the shaggy base of Hawk Butte, when he saw another rider approaching from the gathering shadows.

It was nearly five in the afternoon, the air turning chill. The deputy was cursing the west-falling sun, for nightfall would make tracking Matt Parrish nearly impossible. Nearby, a couple of fighting magpies screeched and ducks chattered in a stream.

McMannigle rode ahead toward the oncoming rider. Soon the wide shoulders, brown bowler, round spectacles, and red mustache, not to mention the medical kit flopping beside his saddle, identified the man as none other than Clyde Evans.

"Say, Doc," McMannigle said as he reined his horse to a halt, "what in the hell are you doing out here?"

"One of Dwayne Creed's boys broke his leg. My buggy's left rear wheel's cracked, or I wouldn't be riding this here cayuse from the livery barn. My ass is still sore from all the ridin' Ben had me do the other day. We must have ridden a good—"

In a hurry to get back after Parrish, McMannigle waved Evans to silence. "I'd love to hear about it, Doc, but I'm after Matt Parrish. He broke jail."

"So that was him," Evans said bemusedly, fingering his mustache.

"You saw him?"

"Several miles south," Evans said. "He was quite a ways off and riding to split the wind. I thought it looked like him, but I couldn't fathom what he'd be doing out of jail and riding an Appaloosa. . . ."

"Which way was he heading?" McMannigle asked, his voice urgent.

"He turned off on that old Army trail that follows the west fork of Little Porcupine Creek."

"Well, he's not heading to his own ranch then," Leon said, thinking it over as he studied Parrish's tracks beneath his steel-dust gelding. Returning his eyes to Evans, he said, "Say, isn't the Little Porcupine Creek trail a shortcut to the Three-Witch?"

"That it is," Evans said, nodding. "I've taken that route a few times when I was in a hurry. It's hairy, though—through a couple canyons, and you don't know who's gonna be out there either. One time I ran into none other than Ed Timron and his brother, Earl—the orneriest pair of—"

"Thanks, Doc," McMannigle said, giving his horse the spurs. "Gotta go."

And then he was off, galloping down the trail.

Evans reined his mouse-brown dun around and galloped after the deputy. "Confound it anyway—wait for me!"

Riding full out, McMannigle tossed a questioning look behind him.

Hunkered over his saddle horn, holding his bowler on his head with one hand, Evans explained, "I've known Matt a long time. I might be able to talk some sense into him, keep him from getting shot!"

Parrish felt fortunate that Alvin Anderson's Appaloosa had been standing across the street from the jail when he'd broken out. The horse had powerful legs and hips and a heart like a locomotive. It could gallop hard for a long distance, and at the moment, heading for Anchor in Three-Witch Valley, Parrish valued nothing more.

He knew Leon McMannigle was probably on his trail by now, and Parrish wanted very much to get to Anchor and make sure Nancy was safe before the deputy caught up to him.

He had a feeling she wasn't safe, though. He had a raw, gnawing feeling in the pit of his stomach that something had gone very wrong out at Anchor, and that Tom Suthern's murder was only one of its results. He suspected that Tommy was the killer and, to get all of Anchor for himself, the young firebrand would kill his sister too.

Parrish spurred the Appaloosa and slapped its rump with his hand, hunkering low in the saddle.

Nancy...

By the time he reined the Appy to a halt in the Anchor compound, the sky was dark and so was the house. He pounded on the door anyway, and as he'd expected, no one answered.

"Who's there?" someone called from near the bunkhouse.

Parrish swung around and realized he'd heard the thuds of a wood mallet when he'd ridden into the compound. The sounds had died as the man chopping wood had given his attention to Parrish.

Parrish jogged toward the bunkhouse, leading the Appy behind him.

"Parrish?" Bernie Sykes said. He stood by the woodpile and chopping block, holding the mallet in both hands and staring at Parrish through the darkness lit by the bunkhouse windows, where the Anchor riders had congregated for the evening. Sykes's eyes hooded suspiciously. "What in the hell are you doin' out of jail?"

Parrish shook his head. There was no time to explain. "Where's Nancy? Where's Miss Suthern?" His breathless, urgent voice betrayed his desperation.

Sykes studied him.

"Come on, Bernie!" Parrish demanded. "I need to know where Nancy is! She could be in danger!"

"She an' Otero rode out of here about an hour ago."

"Which way?"

"They took the main road east."

"You don't know where they were going?"

"She don't tell me nothin'," Sykes said. "But now, you tell me what in the hell you're doin' out of jail. You didn't break and run, did ye?"

But Parrish was already climbing into the saddle and gigging the Appy out of the yard.

"Hey, Parrish," Sykes called. "Get the hell back here an' answer my question!"

The only answer Sykes received was the dwindling thuds

of the Appy's hoofbeats as horse and rider disappeared in the darkness.

When he was out on the main trail, riding east, Parrish's guts churned with dread. He had a bad feeling Otero was taking Nancy onto the range to kill her. Maybe he'd had a gun on her that Sykes hadn't seen, or maybe Otero had lured her into the countryside some other way, with some kind of lie about something she needed to see.

Parrish didn't know—his brain swirled with possibilities—but he would have bet silver cartwheels against horse apples that Nancy was in trouble.

Otero and Tommy were no doubt in cahoots to get all of Anchor for themselves.

Parrish's theory soured considerably, however, when the tracks he'd been following led him to Vasserman's roadhouse an hour later. The cabin was dark and deserted, and the corral was filled with steers wearing freshly doctored brands—brands so fresh, in fact, it was obvious they'd worn the Anchor brand only a few hours ago. The stench of burned hide and hair still fouled the air around the corral, in which the cattle bawled and milled, wary of Parrish.

The rancher dismounted the exhausted Appaloosa and looked around.

What in the hell was going on?

His fear for Nancy's life had been tempered by utter confusion.

Nancy and Otero had ridden away from Anchor only a couple of hours ago. Why? They'd ridden to the roadhouse where a dozen of their rustled beeves had been penned.

Maybe Otero had discovered the rustled cattle and gone back to the ranch for help. But then, why hadn't he taken the other men? Why had Nancy been the only one who'd ridden off with him, when there was a very good chance they'd run into the men who'd stolen her cattle?

Parrish dipped his hands in the stock tank beneath the windmill, splashing his face and massaging his neck. He was bone-weary and more confused than he'd ever been in his life. He felt as though he were lost in some terrible dream in which all his reference points had been scrambled.

Nothing, none of this, made any sense at all. . . .

Far off in the cool, quiet night, a rifle cracked. The swirling echo took a long time dying. Parrish lifted his head, following the sound with his eyes.

It had come from the southeast. He waited, listening, but there were no more reports. Just that one.

Could have been a hunter or a cowboy shooting at wolves. But something told Parrish that wasn't it at all.

The stalwart Appaloosa had moved to the water tank, and was still drawing water as Parrish scrambled into the saddle. In a few seconds, he'd reined the Appy around and was cantering into the glowering darkness of the Three-Witch Valley night, heading for the rifle's bark.

22

THE RIFLE'S CRACK wrenched Stillman out of his stupor. Tied to the saddle of his bay, which Nancy and Otero must have found as they approached the roadhouse, he lifted his chin from his chest. He squinted into the shadows of the woods they were traversing, via a cattle trail winding along a mountainside.

The stars, clear as snow, clung to the treetops.

Two figures stood about thirty feet before him—Nancy and Otero—while another lay writhing on the ground, his cries loud in the silent night. Three horses flanked Nancy and Otero; the rifle's bark had made them jittery.

"Goddamn you . . . goddamn you, sons of bitches," the man on the ground groaned. Stillman recognized Hannabe's voice. Powder smoke wafted around him.

"That's no way to talk to a lady, Dave," Otero admonished.

"No, I'm deeply offended, Dave," said Nancy. "You shouldn't have tried to run off like that."

Hannabe grunted and cursed again. By the way he was lying, arms tied behind him, the bullet must have taken him through the lower back. "You were gonna kill me anyway,"

he said, his voice weakening. He was dying, no doubt about
it.

Stillman's wrists were tied to the saddle horn, tighter
than before. His hands were numb. His feet were tied beneath the belly of the bay.

His head ached so badly that he intermittently saw double. Above him, the stars swooned.

To his left, two horses stood, heads up, pricking their
ears at the commotion. Atop one horse sat Blacklaws. Atop
the other sat the girl. They were both tied like Stillman, but
they were both naked and ghostly pale in the variegated
shadows of the pines.

The girl was hunched over her saddle horn. Stillman
could hear her teeth clacking together. Blacklaws sat stiffly,
apparently fighting the cold with a dogged, sullen determination.

Stillman looked behind him. Vasserman sat another
horse between two pines, starlight reflected on his bullet-
crowned hat and in his horse's wary eyes.

Sliding his gaze forward, Stillman saw Nancy crouch
over Hannabe.

"He dead?" Otero asked her.

"I think so," Nancy replied, straightening, holding a rifle
now. "Throw him over his horse."

"Leave him here. Hell, the wolves will have him de-
voured by sunup."

"No, I'm not taking any chances," Nancy said. "They'll
all go in the cave where they'll never be found."

So that's where they were heading, Stillman thought,
fighting the splintering shudders racking his brain. To a
cave somewhere around Three-Witch Butte. They'd all be
led inside and shot. No one would find them out here, in
this maze of mountains and canyons and pine-covered
slopes, in a cave Nancy had probably discovered as a girl
riding horseback around her father's range, and which probably no one but Nancy herself and a few long-dead Indians
had ever glimpsed.

"How far away?" Otero asked her, mildly annoyed.

"Fifteen, twenty minutes," she said. "Come on, Dom. Get

him on his horse and let's get moving. I'm getting the creeps out here."

Otero yanked Hannabe up by an arm and, crouching, pulled him over his left shoulder. His voice amused, he said, "Creeps?"

"Witches," Nancy said, gazing around as Otero lumbered toward Hannabe's mount. "That's where the valley gets its name from, you know."

"Witches," Otero said, heaving the body over the horse's saddle. He laughed. "You're afraid of witches." He chuckled.

"Shut up, Dom. Let's get moving." Nancy reached for her horse's reins and hurried into the leather. She leveled her Winchester and rode toward Stillman and Vasserman, her voice urgent as she said, "Come on, let's go!"

Blacklaws whipped his head at her, exploding with rage. "Nancy, you goddamn bitch, give me a blanket! I'm *freezin'*!"

"Hold on, Vince. You'll be dead soon."

With that, she smacked the rump of Vasserman's horse with her rifle. The horse jumped and followed Stillman's bay, following Blacklaws, the girl, and the dead Hannabe respectively. When they were all strung out in a line, Nancy rode drag, behind Vasserman. Stillman kept his head down, feigning unconsciousness once again. It would give him time to think and not draw attention to himself if any means of escape should occur to him.

He had a bad feeling, though. They'd tied him good this time. So good, in fact, that he couldn't move his wrists a hair. He could see that the ropes had cut into his skin and that the dark fluid gleaming occasionally in the starlight was blood, but he couldn't feel the cuts.

He was in it pretty deep this time. Pretty goddamn deep.

They'd ridden five minutes when something sounded from the slope rising on their left.

"What was that?" Nancy said behind Vasserman.

At the head of the group, Otero turned his head to regard her over his shoulder. "What was what?"

As if on cue, the noise sounded again. It was a high,

ululating cry. At first, Stillman thought it was a coyote, then an owl. Then, as the cry rose again, arcing off across the night, he realized he didn't know what in the hell it was.

"Oh, God," he heard Nancy exclaim softly behind him.

"Just some animal," Otero said.

He turned to regard Nancy again. Stillman sensed that she'd stopped her horse. Otero did the same, and the horses behind him halted as well.

"It's just a wolf or something," Otero called back to Nancy, growing impatient.

The cry came again. The closest sound Stillman could pin it to was the lament of a lonely mountain lion, but it was too high-pitched for that, and there was too much air under it. As it lifted toward the stars, it seemed to move and arc around the sky like something physical.

"That's no wolf or something," Nancy said.

Otero sat his saddle, facing rearward, toward Stillman, who kept his chin on his chest. But the lawman's eyes were open. He listened for the sound again, hating to admit it even to himself, but the hair along his spine was pricking, and not from the cold air either.

"What then?" Otero said, his voice growing apprehensive.

"I've heard it before . . . a long time ago," Nancy said. "When I was riding out here alone, at night. I've never ridden at night again."

She paused, probably looking around. "Let's go. Hurry, Dom," she urged.

Blacklaws's teeth ceased their clattering as the rancher raged, "Nancy, goddamn you, give me a blanket. I'm so cold my balls are freezin' to the saddle."

Nancy whipped her head to the blond, nude Blacklaws. Stillman couldn't see her expression, but he could sense it, and it wasn't kind. She reined her horse around, rode to the nude rancher, lifted her carbine, and aimed it at his head.

"Now, wait just a minute," Blacklaws groused, his voice taut with fear.

She did not wait. The carbine jumped and barked, geysering smoke and fire. The bullet tore through the right side of Blacklaws's head, spewing blood and brains as it exited the left. Blacklaws twisted to the left, then slumped forward over his hands tied to the saddle horn.

The whore watched in silence as Nancy rode toward her.

"And while I'm at it," Nancy said. She levered the carbine and shot the whore, who slumped like Blacklaws, dead. "Now let's get out of here!"

She smacked the rear of Vasserman's horse once again, and the group filed along the trail, rounding the mountain and spilling into a wooded ravine. Stillman blinked at the slumped bodies of Blacklaws and the whore and indulged in the wry speculation that it was best not to get chatty with a girl like Nancy Suthern.

The eerie cry rose about every two or three minutes, sometimes sounding near, sometimes far, then near again, almost a few yards away. Otero rode point. Nancy smacked Vasserman's horse from behind, urging the group forward at a jolting jog trot that sent arrows through Stillman's tender head.

The trail rose up a steep incline and stopped in a meadow dappled with starlight. Fifty yards away, a slope lifted on Stillman's right, carpeted in deep, dark foliage. Amidst the foliage yawned a cave nearly concealed by brush.

As Sweets ground to a halt behind the horse carrying the dead Hannabe, Stillman realized he hadn't heard the eerie echo for several minutes now.

"Get everybody out of their saddles and into the cave," Nancy called to Otero as she dismounted her own filly in a hurry.

The sound rose again. Brush rustled near the cave. Stillman swung his head in that direction and saw shrubs moving. A figure grew out of them, tall and black. It rose a few feet in the air, wings flapping, then fell to the meadow floor near the cave's entrance with a thud.

A short version of the cry sounded, followed by the unmistakable rasp of a bullet being levered into a rifle's breech.

"Hold it right there, little sister," a man's voice called.

Nancy and Otero had frozen near their horses, obviously befuddled and petrified. Stillman's own heart was hammering a hurried blackmith's beat against his breastbone.

Behind him came the sound of more rustling brush followed by footsteps and cocking rifles.

"Don't make any fast moves, little sister," the man by the cave said. "You neither, Otero, or I'll ventilate you both right here and now."

Stillman heard Nancy's voice catch in her throat. Raspily, unbelievingly, she said, "You . . ."

The eerie witch's cry lifted, followed by Tommy Suthern's unmistakable chuckle. "It's me, little sis. It's been me all along."

"You made those sounds. . . ."

"Does a bear shit in the woods?" Tommy said with a laugh as he strode toward the horses, his black duster flapping around his legs. "It worked to scare the bloomers off you back then, and it works now. Maybe you ain't as almighty smart as you think you are. Like I said, don't make any fast moves; you're covered from behind."

No longer caring who knew he was awake, Stillman turned to see two other men with rifles. One stood behind Nancy, the other behind Otero. The man behind Nancy was grinning. Stillman couldn't see his face in the darkness, but he thought it was Joe Coombs, who had worked for Tom Suthern. The other man was probably also a member of Tommy's owlhoot band.

Mentally, Stillman scratched his jaw. This was getting right interesting. . . .

"Drop those guns," Tommy ordered his sister and Otero.

"Tommy, what do you think you're doing?" Nancy said, growing angry. "This is for us . . . you and me."

"You and me, eh?" Tommy said. "That why you killed the old man before I could convince him to put me back in his will? Before I could convince him you were diddling both Blacklaws and Otero, trying to get them on your side against him and me?"

Tommy Suthern approached his sister stiffly and aimed his Winchester at her belly. With his free hand, he grabbed her rifle and .38 and chucked them off in the grass.

Meanwhile, one of his two cohorts was disarming Otero and prodding him into the meadow, away from his horse.

Tommy shook his head. "Nah, the ranch is all mine, little sister. And when Parrish is dead by the hangman and old Blacklaws has finally kicked the bucket, the whole damn valley will be mine."

The man standing on the other side of Nancy's horse cleared his throat loudly.

"I mean ours," Tommy corrected himself. "Mine and Joe's and Leejay's."

Stillman almost chuckled. So many people were getting screwed in their scramble to secure all of the Three-Witch for themselves that he wondered if anyone but the deer were going to end up with it in the end. He also wondered if the valley wasn't haunted after all. There had to be one hell of a curse on this place.

Nancy shuddered. "You wouldn't kill me, would you . . . little brother?"

"That's what you were gonna do to do me, wasn't it?"

"Of course not," Nancy exclaimed, as if correcting a grave misunderstanding. "Dom and I were going to bring you into our plan, right where you belong. Tommy, you're family. I didn't bring you in before because I didn't think you'd go along with killing Dad."

Tommy chuckled. Mockingly, he said, "You didn't think I'd go along with killing Pa, huh? Psawh! I'd of killed the old bastard myself, if first I coulda wriggled my way back into his will!"

"Tommy, you—"

"Get away from me!" Tommy ordered, taking a step back and lifting his rifle barrel at his sister. "You're gonna die tonight, Sis. Along with all these other no-account bastards. The only one I'm a little sad about killin' is Stillman. I wanted to take him down in a fair fight, just him and me." He grinned. "I'll get over it."

He turned to the rifleman standing closest to him. "Joe, cut the badge-toter loose. Leejay"—he paused to laugh—"get Hannabe and Blacklaws and the girl off their horses

and haul 'em into the cave with Stillman and Vasserman."
He called to the man near Otero. "Send Stillman and Vasserman the way of the other three, then get back out here
and try to cover up these tracks. I don't want anyone cuttin'
all this sign out here, in the off chance anyone ever strays
this far off the main trails."

Stillman's hands ached and prickled as, when they were
finally freed from the tight rope securing them to his saddle
horn, the blood rushed through veins that must have been
pinched to the size of stickpins. He rubbed his wrists and
glanced around.

The man called Leejay had freed the girl, rolling her off
her horse and into the meadow's knee-high grass. Having
cut the ropes tying Blacklaws to his saddle, Leejay gave
the blond nude carcass a shove. Blacklaws tumbled to the
ground in a heap—a pale flash of arms and legs and blond
hair followed by the sound of thrashing brush.

Meanwhile, Joe Coombs bent down to cut the rope connecting Stillman's ankles beneath the belly of his bay.
Without giving it much thought, but knowing he had to do
something fast, Stillman kicked his left foot out savagely
from his stirrup.

Coombs had been straightening after freeing Stillman's
feet, and wasn't ready for the attack. Stillman's boot took
him toe-first in the throat. Grunting and wheezing and dropping his rifle as he grabbed his neck, Coombs stumbled
back in the brush and fell.

Wasting no time and ignoring his pounding head, Stillman flung himself from the saddle, diving toward the rifle
in the grass.

"Hey!" Tommy yelled, ducking to peer under Stillman's
horse.

"Nobody move!" boomed a voice familiar to Stillman's
ears. It rose over the meadow, rending the silence beneath
the stars and freezing everyone, including Stillman himself.

Turning to peer around the meadow, Tommy said with
disbelief, "Who the hell's that?"

23

AGAIN, THE RESONANT voice boomed across the meadow. "I said don't move! We have each one of you sons o' bitches in our sights and are just itchin' to drop the hammers on ye!"

Lying on the ground, Coombs's rifle in his hands, Stillman grinned, feeling a relieved buoyancy in spite of the hammering in his skull. "That, my friend, is Leon McMannigle," he told Tommy. "Deputy sheriff of Hill County and a prime candidate for sainthood, if I have anything to say about it."

Stillman stood and peered around the meadow. Three men had stepped out from the trees, a good distance apart, and were walking slowly across the meadow, long guns extended. From the tall, loose-jointed, broad-shouldered frame, Stillman could tell that the man in the middle was Leon. The blocky man on the deputy's right appeared to be Doc Evans, starlight glinting off his glasses and off the barrel of the double-barreled Greener in his hands.

Who in the hell was the willowy, hatless man on McMannigle's left?

The three men were halfway across the meadow when

Nancy bolted out from behind her brother. Before Stillman had time to react, she'd jumped onto the horse vacated by Vasserman, and ground her spurs into the animal's loins.

"Hee-ya!" she cried.

The surprised horse sprang off its back feet with a whinny, leaping high as it broke into a gallop between Blacklaws and the girl and thundered across the meadow and into the woods, out of sight.

"I got her!" Stillman yelled to Leon as he grabbed Sweets's bridle reins and climbed into the hurricane deck.

In a moment he was following Nancy's path across the meadow and through the trees, ducking under branches that tore and slashed at his face. Gazing ahead through the pines, he spied movement and reined Sweets to the right, onto a game trail that descended the mountain at an angle.

"Come on, boy," Stillman urged the horse, keeping his gaze on the moving shadow ahead. Vagrant light intermittently found Nancy's hat or horse's rump or saddle trimmings.

Following the girl, Stillman descended the mountain, splashed and clattered across a half-frozen stream, and mounted another incline. Sweets traced a circuitous route, following the game trail through trees and brush, leaping deadfalls, descending declivities with jolts that rearranged Stillman's organs and momentarily blinded him as pain spasms racked his tender skull.

It was during one such spasm, as he descended a narrow ravine, that he caught a glimpse of movement to his right. Before he could gather his senses, something hard smacked his shoulder. The attack was so sudden and unexpected that Stillman felt the reins jerked out of his hands.

Then he was stretched out across Sweets's left flank and becoming airborne as the horse galloped out from beneath him. The ground sprang up hard and, grunting with the violent meeting of his backside with juniper shrubs, he rolled down a hill, coming finally to rest on his back.

He didn't feel so much pain as suffocation, as though his lungs were pinched taut, allowing no breath. He grunted and wheezed, trying to gulp at the cold night air.

Blinking at the star-dusted sky yawning above the silhouetted pine tops, he saw a shadow enter his vision. It was Nancy Suthern, hatless, hair mussed and tumbling across her shoulders, still holding the branch with which she'd clubbed Stillman off his horse.

Her eyes were flat and cold.

Only half-consciously, Stillman reflected that he would have been happier to see a grizzly bear. This girl had more pluck and devil's dance than half the men he'd tangled with in his long career—a career he seemed bound and determined to let this kill-crazy vixen bring to an end.

Nancy dropped the club with a thud. She moved her arm, brought it up. In her hand, something flashed dully. A small gun, Stillman saw. A double-barreled derringer she must have had in her coat pocket.

There was a ratchety click as she thumbed the hammer back.

Stillman reflected automatically, with an ethereal objectivity, upon Fay's wish to have a baby. And then he heard, as if from another world: "Nancy."

The voice came from behind her, in front of Stillman. It wheeled her around. Stillman wanted to take the opportunity to dive for her legs, but his limbs would not respond. The bullet a drunk whore had fired into his back many years ago was barking loudly now—it was snugged too close to his spine for the doctors to risk removing it—and only a trickle of air had found its way into his lungs.

"Matt—?"

"Put the gun down, Nancy."

She didn't say anything. Stillman wondered how Parrish had gotten out of jail, but was damn glad he had. At the moment, the sheriff felt as helpless as a landed fish.

"I won't," she said mildly, matter-of-factly.

Stillman heard Parrish slowly approaching through the trees, his boots crunching leaves and raking stones. "Don't make me shoot you, Nancy. I love you, fool that I am."

"How did you know?" she asked.

Parrish stopped. "It was pretty damn obvious when Leon and the doc and I caught up to you a few miles back." He shook his head, bunching his lips with pain. "You're something else—you know that? All sugar and spice on the outside, and pure venom within."

"Matt, I—"

"No more of your goddamn lies!" Parrish yelled. He paused, then said with a chuff, "You and Otero . . ." After another pause, his voice leveled, but the anger was still there. "You got me to fall in love with you, and then you framed me for murder. Blacklaws was in on it too. That's why he did his damnedest to goad me into a fight the other day, to remind everyone what a hothead I was, how capable I was of murder. Only he didn't realize you and Otero . . . well, you know."

Parrish smiled, but it was more of a grimace.

"They're all just fools," she said.

"And I was the biggest fool of all."

"I could have loved you," she said speculatively.

"If I'd been able to convince your father to sell to me maybe. But you would have wanted the Copper Kettle too, and I wouldn't have had any interest in expanding that far. I'm not that ambitious. Or greedy."

Her voice was cold. "I know."

"But now you won't have any of it," Parrish said. "You didn't count on being double-crossed by Blacklaws, who was stealing your beef to ruin you, as bad as you were double-crossing him." He chuckled without mirth. "All this treachery. For nothing."

Regaining his wind, Stillman sat up. Nancy's back was to him. In front of her, he saw Matt Parrish's silhouette, gun extended in his hand. Nancy held her derringer down at her side.

"That's the way I'd want it," she said simply, her voice taut. "All or nothing."

"Nancy, don't!"

She swung the derringer up, but Parrish fired before she could pull the pocket pistol's trigger. She jerked, took half a step back, froze there, and fired the derringer into the ground.

She gave a soft, groaning wheeze and dropped to her

knees. She dropped the derringer and brought her hands to her belly, lowered her head to look at the wound.

She looked at Parrish. Stillman saw her jaw move, trying to speak, but no words came out.

"I'm sorry, Nancy," Parrish said, genuine grief in his voice. Smoke curled from the barrel of his extended Colt.

She sat there on her knees for several seconds, her breath growing short. Then she gave a final sigh and flopped over on her back, hair spilling out around her head as she died.

The young rancher lowered his gun and walked heavy-footed to the dead girl. He stared down at her. Finally, he dropped to his knees, lowered his head, and sobbed.

24

THE NEXT TUESDAY evening, Clyde Evans drove his black buckboard wagon, which did double duty as a hearse, over to Katherine Kemmett's neat little house on the south side of Clantick. He reined his lumbering horse, Faustus, up to the hitch rack, set the brake, and dismounted.

He looked around self-consciously, straightened his bowler and his cravat, flicked lint from the arm of his freshly laundered suit jacket, and started through the gate in the picket fence. Remembering something, he stopped, returned to the wagon, and grabbed the flowers from under the seat. They were a collection of autumnals, including cattails and red-leafed sumac branches, he'd picked from the ravine below his house and had wrapped in fancy sienna paper he'd purchased at the mercantile.

Flowers in hand, he strolled through the gate, mounted the porch, and knocked on the door. Waiting, he glanced around again self-consciously, nodded to the Widow Bjornson peering out the parlor window of the house next door, and straightened his jacket. Inside, footsteps sounded.

The door opened. Evans's stomach fluttered as Katherine

Kemmett appeared, looking mildly surprised, her hair wrapped in an elegant bun and secured with an indigo pin. "Why, Clyde," she said in her characteristically mocking tone, "how punctual of you."

"Please let me in," he said tightly. "We're being spied upon."

Katherine stuck her head out the door, turned to regard the Widow Bjornson still peering out her lace-curtained window, and waved. "Oh, that's just the widow looking out for my welfare. I don't think she trusts you, Clyde." Katherine chuckled huskily.

"She's being nosy, Katherine," Evans said. "And I feel ridiculous holding these flowers. Let me in."

"Oh, how lovely!" Katherine exclaimed as she stepped back, drawing the door wide. As Evans followed her over the threshold, she accepted the arrangement, cooing, "An autumn spray. How I love autumn foliage. Oh, Clyde, you shouldn't have!"

Pleased with himself, Evans rose up on the balls of his feet and flushed. "It was really nothing. I found them all in the ravine below my house."

Katherine closed the door, then turned and walked toward the kitchen. "Let me get these in a vase right away, and I'll set them on the mantel."

The doctor felt awkward, not quite sure what to do with himself, his mind more than partly on the prospect of sleeping with Katherine later. She looked more desirable than usual in her white, formfitting dress with ruffled sleeves and gold buttons. He stood in the parlor doorway rolling the brim of his bowler. As she dropped the flowers in the vase she'd filled with water, he couldn't help giving her nicely curving backside a quick, furtive appraisal. He quickly lifted his gaze, however, when Katherine turned around.

"Thanks so much, Clyde. I love having autumn flowers, but I just haven't had time to pick any for myself."

Evans gave a humble shrug, inwardly pleased she liked the gift.

She smiled as she strode to him, rose up on her toes, and

pecked his cheek. "Now you just have a seat in that comfortable chair over there. There's a drink already waiting for you on the table with the plant. I'll have supper ready in fifteen minutes."

Evans's eyes roamed to the drink—a brandy, no doubt—in a short, yellow glass. Saliva collected on his tongue. "That's . . . very nice, Katherine."

He hadn't expected to be offered liquor here. What a nice surprise. She really did like him; that much was obvious. He just hoped she followed through with her intimated promise to sleep with him. Evans wasn't sure why he wanted to sleep with her so badly. He could sleep with a whore any time he wanted—women sexier than Katherine, and probably a lot better versed in pleasing the male of the species.

He guessed it was the challenge of Katherine that drew him to her, her being the rather persnickety widow of a Lutheran minister. Beyond their medical practices, they had little, if anything, in common. He wasn't sure he even really liked her.

He hooked his hat on the metal tree by the door, sat down in the hide-covered rocker, and plucked his drink off the table. As he sipped the brandy, trying not to take too big a drink—he'd probably only get one—the question persisted: Why was he here when he could be with a whore at Mrs. Lee's place or at Serena's Pleasure Palace?

A whore would be so much less complicated. He wouldn't have to endure the small talk over a meal, and he wouldn't have to voice the usual platitudes over her cooking. He could drink as much as he wanted.

And he wouldn't have this damn fluttering in his gut. What were those anyway, those confounded butterflies? Why did he feel like a damn schoolboy on his first date of the summer? He was here to tumble. Nothing more. If he wasn't tumbled, he'd light out for a whorehouse. It was as simple as that.

Brows furrowed with consternation, he took another sip of the drink and sat back in the chair, waiting for the brandy to quell the butterflies in his gut.

"You can sit up now, Clyde," Katherine called from the kitchen as he reluctantly took the last swallow of his drink.

"Not a minute too soon," he said to himself, climbing out of the chair.

The supper was delicious—a roast from the hog a local farmer had butchered only yesterday. Katherine served it with green beans from her garden, fresh-baked bread slathered in butter and currant jelly, and mashed potatoes with pork gravy slightly blackened the way Evans liked it. She followed the main meal up with apple cobbler and a liberal dollop of whipped cream from Mrs. Bjornson's milch cow, and strong, black coffee brewed with eggshells—again, the way Evans liked it.

Yep, the woman fancied him, the doctor thought as he sat back and wiped his mouth and mustache with his napkin. There was no doubt about that.

The question was: Did he like her?

Well, he'd probably have a better idea about that tomorrow morning, he thought with an inward chuckle.

But then the confounded butterflies started fluttering once more, and for a moment his vision swam.

"Would you like an after-dinner drink, Clyde?"

Skeptically, he looked at Katherine smiling across her empty plate. Would he? "Well, if you're offering . . ."

"The bottle's up there," she said, glancing at the cabinet above the icebox. "Help yourself. You can take it to the living room, and I'll be there when I've finished the dishes."

"Do you need any help?" he heard himself ask, not sure where the question had come from. He had never considered himself a man who would help a woman with supper dishes.

"No, but thank you. That's very sweet."

While she busied herself clearing the table, Evans poured himself a liberal jigger of brandy, noting how his hand shook slightly, jostling the bottle against the glass. He glanced at Katherine, wondering if she'd noticed, but her back was to him, and she did not turn around.

Confound it anyway, he thought as he retreated to the

living room. What was happening to him? He had half a mind to say he had a headache and flee to Serena's. But something would not let him go. Something made him sit in Katherine's parlor, sipping his brandy, which he only vaguely enjoyed, and feeling his hands sweat into the arms of his chair.

His cravat was fairly strangling him when Katherine appeared suddenly in the parlor door. She stood there for several seconds, bemusedly, before she suddenly smiled and held out her hand. At first, he wasn't sure what she meant, but then he realized she was holding out her hand for him to take.

His heart performed a catapult, and he cleared his throat and struggled heavily up from his chair. He set down his drink and walked to her, his feet feeling heavy as blacksmith anvils, and took her hand.

She squeezed his hand, gazed into his eyes, smiling, then turned and led him down the short, dark hall. She turned into a room in which a single lantern burned, casting its glow upon a bed with a colorful spread, an oak dresser, a table trimmed with a lace cloth and a photograph of her deceased husband, and a ladder-back chair with a padded seat.

Evans followed her haltingly inside. When she turned to him, her eyes uncharacteristically demure, he placed his hands on her shoulders, drew her to him, and kissed her.

The first time he'd kissed her, he'd been drunk, and she'd pulled brusquely away from him, seemingly horrified by his lusty behavior. Now, however, she pressed her lips gently against his, returning his kiss, and placed her hands on his ruddy cheeks caressingly, lovingly.

Evans's butterflies ceased their frantic flight, and he felt a warming calm seep through him as he drew Katherine even closer. Her mouth, always so straight and prim and seemingly ready to turn down in a reprimanding frown, felt warm and moist and sweet to his own lips. Caressing her shoulders, he felt her body melt into his, the muscles in her back and hips and legs giving up their customary restraint.

Katherine removed her hands from his face, set them flat

against his shoulders, and gently pulled away. She looked into his eyes, smiling subtly, then turned away, walked over to the table upon which the photograph of her late husband sat. She swiveled the picture toward the window, then turned again to the doctor, the tender smile still softening her mouth, making her look, Evans decided, downright lovely.

Suddenly, he heard himself speak, surprised at the words. "Are you sure, Katherine?"

She gazed back at him for a long time, her eyes bright and moist and sparkling in the buttery glow from the lamp. "Oh, Clyde," she said at last, her voice barely above a whisper.

"What is it?"

Her lips jerked as she seemed to fight a sob. "You care how I feel."

He gazed back at her, vaguely surprised at himself. Yes, he realized. He cared how she felt. He did not want her to regret this night. He wanted it to be right for them both.

Odd how that was suddenly important to him. It had never been important to him before, with any of the other women he'd slept with. It was a good feeling, if an alien and slightly startling one, as if he were somehow sharing the emotions of another man—a man who, for the first time in his life, was acquiring the ability to empathize and to love.

He'd never felt so un-alone.

Katherine moved to the bed and slowly drew back the covers. She stood back from the bed, removed her barrette, and let her hair fall about her shoulders.

Several weeks later, the trouble in Three-Witch Valley was becoming a distant memory. The primary instigators had settled into the state pen at Deer Lodge, Nancy Suthern was buried beside her father, and Matt Parrish was running both his own ranch and Anchor.

Doc Evans walked into the sheriff's office with a self-satisfied smirk curling his brushy red mustache.

"What the hell are you smiling about?" Stillman said,

looking up from his desk as the doctor closed the jailhouse door.

Leon McMannigle sat in a chair near the wood stove, which was stoked to glowing. A wintery cold had settled over the town, frosting the office windows.

Cleaning his Spencer repeater with an oily rag, the deputy said to Stillman, "He sure isn't grinning 'cause he's flush—I know that. Last night at Mrs. Lee's, I cleaned him down to his spurs. He crawled home with his pockets inside out!"

McMannigle and Stillman shared a laugh.

Evans rolled his eyes and sat in the Windsor chair before Stillman's desk. The sheriff leaned back in his own swivel chair and regarded the doctor appraisingly. "No, I'd say it's a woman," he speculated.

"A woman?" Leon said. "Why would he be smiling over a woman? He gets women all the time."

"No, this is one *certain* woman," Stillman said. "This isn't just any woman over at one of the whorehouses."

"Come to think of it," Leon said, frowning at the doctor, "he didn't frolic with any of the ladies at Mrs. Lee's place last night, like he usually does. You know how he usually gets one or two to playing slap and tickle with him between poker hands? There wasn't none of that."

Stillman grinned. "It must be love. . . ."

Scowling, Evans sighed. "All right," he said fatefully, getting up from his chair. "Have it your way."

"Have what my way?"

"I'm not going to tell you what I came to tell you if you're gonna sit there and rib me all afternoon." Donning his hat, Evans strolled to the door.

"Okay, Doc." Stillman turned to Leon. "I reckon Mrs. Kemmett is out-of-bounds from now on, Deputy."

"I reckon."

"Sorry, Doc," Stillman said. He still couldn't quite get over the fact that, from all appearances, Evans's relationship with Katherine Kemmett had evolved to something more than professional. Not that he wasn't pleased. Evans had never seemed happier. "What's on your mind?"

Evans stopped near the door and turned casually. "Well, I was just going to let you know how my meeting with your wife went this afternoon is all, but since you're more interested in my personal life, I guess I'll just let Fay tell you herself. . . ."

Stillman froze, blinked once. "Fay? Tell me what?"

"No, no," Evans said. "You'll have to hear the good news from her, I'm afraid. You and your deputy there have done rubbed my fur in the wrong direction."

Stillman's throat was dry. His heart was drumming. "Is she . . . is she . . ."

With haughty indignation, Evans pursed his lips and shrugged. He glanced at the rafters and whistled coyly.

Stillman bolted out of his chair. Without even grabbing his hat or his coat, he flew past Evans and outside, leaving the door hanging wide behind him.

Inside the jailhouse, Evans and McMannigle listened to the sheriff's boots pounding off down the frozen street.

Still whistling, Evans glanced at Leon, smirking. Then he strolled casually outside and closed the door behind him.

Leon stared at the door, his face lit with a toothy grin.

ABOUT THE AUTHOR

Like Louis L'Amour, **Peter Brandvold** was born and raised in North Dakota. He's lived in Arizona, Montana, and Minnesota, and currently resides in the Rocky Mountains near Fort Collins, Colorado. Since his first book, *Once a Marshal*, was published in 1998, he's become popular with both readers and critics alike. His writing is known for its realistic characters, authentic historical details, and lightning-fast pace. Visit his website at www.peterbrandvold.com. Drop him a line at pgbrandvold@msn.com.

PETER BRANDVOLD
series featuring Sheriff Ben Stillman

PETER BRANDVOLD